"Don't use sex as a weapon, Casey. It's all wrong."

Reid pulled her into his arms. "I want to love you more than anything else in the world. To touch you and say your name. To feel your body against mine."

"No! Don't—touch me." With supreme effort, Casey tore herself out of Reid's arms. "You're a liar!" she yelled. "You say that you want us to be lovers more than anything else in the whole world. But it isn't true. If it were, you'd want it more than you want to race. But you won't give up racing so it can't be true."

"Typical feminine logic," Reid growled. "I suppose I'm a fool to think that you'd understand. You're too young." Shoving his hands into his pockets, he turned away.

"Not too young to know that I don't want you to get killed," Casey said as a great sob tore through her.

SALLY WENTWORTH began her publishing career at a Fleet Street newspaper in London, where she thrived in the hectic atmosphere. After her marriage, she and her husband moved to rural Hertfordshire, where Sally had been raised. Although she worked for the publisher of a group of magazines, the day soon came when her own writing claimed her energy and time. Her romance novels are often set in fascinating foreign locales.

Books by Sally Wentworth

Don't miss any of our special offers. Write to us at the following address for information on our newest releases.

Harlequin Reader Service
901 Fuhrmann Blvd., P.O. Box 1397, Buffalo, NY 14240
Canadian address: P.O. Box 603,
Fort Erie, Ont. L2A 5X3

SALLY WENTWORTH

ultimatum

Harlequin Books

TORONTO • NEW YORK • LONDON
AMSTERDAM • PARIS • SYDNEY • HAMBURG
STOCKHOLM • ATHENS • TOKYO • MILAN

Harlequin Presents first edition September 1988
ISBN 0-373-11109-6

Original hardcover edition published in 1987
by Mills & Boon Limited

CHAPTER ONE

IT had been one hell of a day! Casey Everett peered out of the rain-splashed window of the commuter train at the electric lights that glowed in the darkness, trying to make out whether she was near her station yet, but nothing looked familiar. She sat back with a sigh, wishing she was home. Just about everything that could go wrong, had gone wrong today. First her car wouldn't start, and by the time she had got to the station the car park was full, so that in desperation she'd just left the car and run to catch the train. But of course she'd missed it, and this in turn had made her late for a whole series of appointments that she had set up with the heads of buying departments of several big London stores, the last one of which had kept her waiting until after the store had closed before he would see her. And then, to really put the cap on an entirely dismal day, there had been a breakdown on the line and she had had to wait for almost an hour before it had been put right and her train had come in.

What she would most like to do now, Casey decided, was to get home, have a hot bath, then go straight to bed and forget that today had ever existed.

The train slowed and drew into her station at last. Several other passengers, all looking as fed up with British Rail as she was, also got out and queued to hand in their tickets before hurrying out of the station. Casey

followed them, waiting at the traffic lights to cross the
road to the station car park. The rain had stopped, but
the night air felt damp and cold. She had parked—
abandoned, almost—her old car at the far end of the car
park after being unable to find a space anywhere.
Although there were plenty of spaces now; most of the
commuters had retrieved their cars and driven home,
leaving the place empty until tomorrow. There were just
the few people who had been delayed by the breakdown
as she had, and they were hurrying away. There were
just two cars left at the very far end, her own and the one
in front of it, which had its nose parked against the
boundary wall. Casey's footsteps slowed and her heart
began to sink as she only now remembered that she had
parked so closely behind the other car that it had no
chance of getting out.

Oh no! She groaned inwardly, just hoping against
hope that the other driver hadn't got back yet and she
would just be able to drive away. But she might have
known that today of all days she wasn't going to be that
lucky. As she drew nearer she could see a man sitting in
the other car and, as it became apparent that she was
heading in his direction, he got out, shut the door and
leaned against it with his arms folded, watching her.

She took a few more faltering steps forward and then
stopped. Even though he was leaning against his car the
man looked very tall, and there was an aura of angry
menace about him that made Casey suddenly feel afraid.
'I—er . . . is this . . .?' Her voice dried in her throat.

The man moved forward from a block of shadow into
the weak light given by the street lamp, and Casey
gulped. He wore a black patch over his right eye, giving

him a strangely piratical appearance. And right now he was a very irate man indeed.

'I suppose I should have known it would be a female,' he observed in scathing anger. 'Do you realise, woman, that I've been waiting for over an hour for you to move this damn car?'

'I'm sorry. There was a breakdown on the line, or——'

'You shouldn't have parked it there in the first place,' the pirate cut in furiously. 'If you hadn't arrived by this train I would have called the police and had it towed out of the way.'

The fact that he was entirely in the right and she in the wrong made Casey feel guilty, but perversely that made her angry. 'If it hadn't been for the rotten train breaking down I'd have been here ages ago and you'd never have known anything about it,' she retorted.

He gave her a contemptuous look, a look somehow made even more derisive by that eye-patch. 'Typical female reasoning,' he said acidly. 'Well, now that you *are* here, how about moving your damn car out of the way?'

Casey gave him a tight-lipped glance, and fumbled around in her bag for her keys, had a moment of blinding panic when she couldn't find them, but gave a sigh of relief as her fingers closed over them at last. Then, of course, she dropped them on the ground.

The pirate made a very audible sound of exasperation, but made no effort to help her as she groped for them, getting her gloved hand soaking wet in a puddle.

'Er—do you have a torch?' she had to ask eventually.

With a muttered imprecation he jerked open his car door, reached across to the parcel shelf and took out a big, powerful flashlight, which revealed the keys half under the car and in the deepest part of the puddle. Taking off her glove this time, Casey fished them out and he held the torch while she found the right key and inserted it in the lock.

'At last. Now perhaps we can get going!'

He walked back towards his car while Casey hurriedly got into hers and put the key in the ignition, wanting nothing more than to get away from the horrible, bad-tempered ... The key turned, the engine gave a sad, whining sound—and died. Casey stared at the dashboard speechlessly, unable to believe it. Frantically she tried again, but this time the engine didn't even make a sound. Oh no! Not this, too.

Her door opened and the pirate stood there, tall and blackly menacing in his dark overcoat. 'Having trouble?' he asked in a voice of deceptive calm that heralded a full scale thunderstorm.

'It—er ... the battery seems to be flat,' Casey admitted weakly, mentally cowering from his anger.

'The battery is flat, is it?' he repeated, again in that mild tone. 'And did you by any remote chance leave your lights on this morning?'

'Why no, of course not. I . . .' Casey's voice trailed off as she realised that the light switch was in the 'on' position. Slowly she lifted apprehensive eyes to look at him.

The pirate's jaw tightened and then he let rip with the full force of his anger. 'Of all the stupid, forgetful, feeble-minded idiot females it has ever been my misfortune to meet, you take first prize, lady. Not only do you park where you're not supposed to, but then you don't even have the sense to turn off your lights. I have never ...'

But Casey had had enough. Pushing open the door, she

got out, put her hands on her hips and faced up to him.
'How dare you speak to me like that? Anyone could have
forgotten to turn their lights off and have their battery go
flat. I was in one hell of a hurry this morning and I . . .'

'Couldn't be bothered to look for a proper parking
space,' the pirate finished for her. 'Dear God, save me
from all brainless females,' he said scathingly. 'And now I
suppose you expect me to push your car out of the way?'

Casey realised that was true and hastily bit back the
extremely nasty comment she had been about to make.
'Er—yes, please.'

He gave her a glowering look. 'You do realise that
you're parked so close behind me that there's no room to
get in between the two cars?'

It was such an obvious comment that Casey took it as a
rhetorical question and stood in silence while the rotten
man made the most of her discomfiture. Then, with
something like a snarl of annoyance, he took off his well
cut overcoat, revealing an equally good suit. 'Do you
think you might just, possibly, be capable of taking off
the handbrake?' he asked sarcastically.

Casey glared at him, but did as he asked while he
climbed on to the boot of his car and put his feet against
the front of hers.

'OK?'

'Yes, it's off.'

'It had better be.' He braced himself and she could see
the muscles in his legs as he exerted his strength. Hastily
she ran to the side of her car and began to push too. The
car rocked a little but didn't move.

Panting, the pirate relaxed. 'Are you sure you let the
handbrake off?' he asked suspiciously.

'Yes, of course. Look for yourself if you don't believe me,' she added antagonistically.

He did too, climbing down to have a look inside the car, and then walking round it. When he got to the back he groaned. 'No wonder I couldn't shift the darn thing; the back wheel is in a deep pothole.'

Casey went round to look, not daring to say a word in case he really lost his temper. 'Look round for a piece of wood,' he ordered shortly.

Where on earth was she supposed to find that? Casey looked about her rather helplessly, then gingerly groped her way into a piece of rough ground that lay between the car park and a small river that cut deep into the ground. She could have done with the torch, but the pirate, of course, had taken that for himself and was searching along beside the wall. Her foot slipped in some mud and she struggled to retain her balance, her ankles catching against something that projected from the ground. 'Ouch. Oh, hell!' Her tights had caught on the thing and she bent to free them, but in the end had to just pull, leaving a big hole. And they were new tights, too. Damn the man, she thought, perversely blaming the pirate. But when her hand touched it, she found that the object was a piece of wood and she gave a cry of triumph. 'I've found something,' she called.

The torchlight came hurrying back and the pirate examined her find. 'Hm. It looks pretty solid. Let's just hope it's strong enough. Here, hold the torch.' After two or three heaves the plank came free from the earth that half covered it and he carried it over to wedge it under her back wheel. 'OK, let's have another go.'

This time he took off his jacket too, but as he climbed up

on to the boot it began to rain again, large spots that soon soaked through the thin material of his shirt. He cursed and began to push, Casey adding her slender strength, and this time the car really began to move. His muscles straining, the pirate made one last tremendous effort and the car came up out of the pothole, leaving enough space for them to get between the cars. He slid to the ground, his chest under the damp material heaving from the exertion.

He stood there for a moment, getting his breath back, and Casey turned to look at him, realising that he must be immensely strong to have moved the car. He was tall, about six feet two inches, but his overcoat and jacket had disguised the broadness of his chest and the strength in his arms and shoulders.

Feeling her eyes on him he turned his head to return her look, his left eyebrow rising sardonically. 'Seen enough?' he asked jeeringly.

Casey drew herself up. 'I'm afraid you're getting awfully wet,' she said huffily.

The pirate gave a harsh laugh. 'Wet. Cold. Splashed with mud. Dirty. You name it. And all because of you,' he told her derisively. 'Come on, one more push should get it out of the way.'

They pushed again, and as her car was none too clean, they both got greasy as well.

'Good, I should be able to get my car out now.' Shrugging himself into his jacket, the pirate got into his car, started the engine and manoeuvred it away from the wall.

Casey watched, getting steadily wetter and wetter. Then she had a sudden fear and ran forward. 'You're not going to *leave* me here, are you?' she wailed.

The electronically controlled window purred down and the pirate looked at her. 'Charming as I find your company,' he told her mendaciously, 'I have absolutely no wish to continue our acquaintance.'

'But you can't just drive away and leave me here like this. What about my car?'

He looked across to where her old estate car stood forlornly under the lamp. 'Well, if you really want my advice—I'd push it in the river and forget all about it.'

'Why, you . . .'

But he held up a hand before she could really let fly at him. 'But as I see that it's evidently your pride and joy, I'll stop at the nearest garage and tell them to send a mechanic round with some jump leads to get you started.' He lifted a dirt-stained hand in farewell. 'Goodbye, lady. Somehow I just can't feel that it was nice meeting you.'

He drove away then, his wheels splashing her as he went past, and Casey looked after him angrily, watching his tail-lights as he drove across the huge car park to the entrance, out of sight on the other side. Glumly she turned away and got into her car to wait for the mechanic, wondering when on earth she would get home that night. Her hair was wet and she felt thoroughly miserable, so that it was a small miracle when a car pulled up beside her only ten minutes or so later. Quickly she got out and walked over to it. 'Thanks for coming so quickly. My battery's flat and I . . .' Her voice trailed off as the other car's window wound down and she saw the pirate's now familiar face looking out at her. 'You—er—came back?'

'Yes.' Parking his car against the wall again, he got out

and took out a briefcase and his overcoat, swinging the latter over his broad shoulders.

'W-what happened?'

With tight-lipped menace, he turned to face her. 'They lock the car park at nine o'clock. That's what's happened.'

Casey stared at him blankly. 'You—you mean—we're locked in?'

'That's exactly what I mean. Because of your incredible thoughtlessness and stupidity, I can't even get home now that my car is free,' he told her with scarcely contained anger.

'But surely there must be someone who has a key? The station—the man in the ticket office must have it.'

'He doesn't. That was the first place I tried. It seems that the man in charge of the car park takes the key home with him every night. And no,' he added before she had a chance to interrupt, 'it is impossible to get in touch with him at home because the ticket seller happens to know that he always goes out on Wednesday nights and he could be in one of a dozen places. So,' he paused eloquently, 'thanks to you, our cars will have to stay here for the night. And we'll just have to hope that they don't get vandalised. Not that you would be likely to notice with that heap you call a car,' he added sneeringly.

'You don't have to be so downright nasty,' Casey told him angrily. 'It happens to be the best I can afford.'

Her voice had risen and he gave her a sharp look. 'I beg your pardon.'

She calmed down at once. 'It—it's OK. Look, I'm sorry about all this. I really am.' He didn't answer and she asked unhappily, 'What do we do now?'

'Try and get a couple of taxis, I suppose. Unless you have someone you can phone to come and pick you up?'

'No.' Casey shook her head. 'I live alone.'

'A taxi it is, then. Come on, there's a pub half a mile down the road. We might as well phone from there.'

Casey collected her things from the car and began to walk along beside him, their feet splashing in the puddles. For the life of her she couldn't think of anything to talk about—anything that wouldn't make him angry again, that was—so they walked along in a grim sort of silence, Casey having to hurry to keep up with his long strides.

The lights of the Axe and Compass looked more than welcoming. Casey gave a sigh of relief as she stepped inside out of the rain and went to stand in front of the big log fire that burned in the saloon bar. Her companion went to speak to the barman and then came over. 'I've got the number of a local taxi firm. I'll order a taxi for you at the same time, if you'll tell me where you want to go to.'

'Thanks. To Barham Ford,' Casey told him, naming a small hamlet a few miles north of the town. He nodded and walked away while Casey went over to the bar to order a couple of double whiskies, then carried them over to a table near the fire. She took off her coat, but her hair and feet were soaked. Casey grimaced as she caught sight of herself in an etched mirror on the wall; her long blonde hair, which she had carefully blow-dried early that morning, had now gone into a mass of curls that clung to her head and dripped down on to the shoulders of her sweater. And her feet looked terrible; her shoes covered in mud, her legs splashed and dirty, and a big hole in her tights where she had caught them on the piece of wood. Yeuk! Casey hated not to be clean and tidy, and could quite happily have burst into tears. Instead she sat down at the table and took a large swig of the whisky, which didn't make her look any better but certainly made her feel a whole lot warmer.

Looking up, she saw the pirate come back into the bar and her hand stayed poised in mid-air. She hadn't really looked at him as a person before, but now he stood under the bright electric light and she was able to take a really good look at him. He didn't seem quite so menacing any more; there were no shadows to harden the planes of his lean face, and his hair was shown to be a dark brown and not black as she had thought. It looked as if it would be thick, too, once it had dried. But he had a hard face, his jaw, beneath his thin-lipped mouth, had the strong thrust of determination. He looked like a man who was used to getting his own way—and who was quite capable of ruthlessness if he was crossed. But perhaps it was only the black patch over his eye that made him seem like that. Who knew, without it he might have given an entirely different impression. But his body was lean and hard so he would always be strongly attractive, and hand-some too, but for that one flaw. He walked across the room to join her, and Casey couldn't help wondering just what had happened to his eye.

But she tried to keep the curiosity out of her face, saying brightly, 'I thought we might have time for a quick drink. I hope you like whisky.'

'Thank you, yes. But you really shouldn't have.'

'Oh, nonsense. It was the least I could do in the—er—circumstances,' Casey protested.

Sitting down beside her, he said wryly, 'There's no point in hurrying over your drink; we're going to have to wait some time for a taxi. The firm only have two in operation this evening because of illness among their drivers, and both of those are out on calls with more people waiting.'

'Oh, no!' Casey lifted appalled eyes to meet his.

He grinned rather satanically. 'Turning out to be quite a night, isn't it?' he agreed.

'But surely there must be other taxi firms?'

He shook his head. 'I tried the only other one in the book, but they're in an even worse position; two of their taxis have been booked by people on an outing to London and won't be back till gone midnight, and one of the others has broken down, so their remaining cab had to go and help. So I'm afraid we'll just have to wait here until one becomes free.'

Lifting his glass, he took a drink of whisky as if he needed it and then turned to look at her, studying her much as she had looked at him earlier. Suddenly becoming extremely conscious of her appearance, Casey picked up her big hold-all-type handbag and, with a muttered, 'Excuse me,' went out to the ladies' cloakroom. As she had hoped, there was a hot-air hand-drier there and she was able to crouch beneath it and dry her hair, fluffing it up until it shone in a golden aureole of soft curls around her head. Next she washed her legs and cleaned her shoes, then re-did her make-up, afterwards stepping back to look at herself in the mirror. Yes, that was better. With her straight black skirt and thin-knit pearl-grey sweater, she looked almost presentable again. Not as good as she'd have liked to have looked while having a drink with a man as arrantly masculine as the pirate, but still ... It would have to do, anyway.

Drawing herself up to her full five feet eight inches, Casey left the cloakroom and went back into the bar, pausing in the doorway as some people were coming out. The pirate looked across and saw her, and rose slowly to his feet, his eyes openly looking her over as she walked towards him. His left eyebrow lifting in surprise, he said, 'Quite a transformation.'

Taking that as a compliment—after all, what else could it be after the way she had looked?—Casey smiled and said, 'It's nice to be dry again. But what about you? Your shirt was soaked.'

He looked amused. 'Well, I can hardly take it off and dry it,' he pointed out sardonically. But added, 'Don't worry. I'm used to getting wet. It will soon dry on me.'

Casey nodded and picked up her glass to drink, but was aware that he was watching her.

'Perhaps we ought to introduce ourselves, as we're likely to be here for some time,' he suggested. 'My name's Lomax, Reid Lomax.'

Casey almost said 'How do you do,' but felt that it was a bit late in the circumstances, so she merely answered, 'Mine's Casey Everett.'

'An unusual name,' he commented. 'And you live at Barham Ford, I think you said? That's a tiny place a couple of miles off the main road, isn't it?'

'Yes, there are only a few houses and farms there. No shops or pub or anything.'

Reid gave her an appraising look. 'That's rather a lonely place for a young girl to live alone, surely? But perhaps you work in London?'

'No.' She shook her head, her fair hair catching the light. 'No, actually I work at home. I didn't particularly choose Barham Ford to live in, but it was the only place I could find that had a suitable workroom attached to the house.'

His left eyebrow rose questioningly, but Casey suddenly found it strangely unnerving to be able to see only half of his expression and she didn't go on, so he had to prompt her. 'And what work do you do?' he asked, his mouth twisting into a thin smile of self-mockery as if he guessed her thoughts.

'I—I design knitwear. Like this sweater I'm wearing.' His eyes—no, his one eye—moved to look over her and Casey flushed slightly, hurrying to add, 'That's why I went up to London today; to try and get some orders. But my car wouldn't start and I was late, so I . . .'

He smiled in amusement as her voice faded off and Reid said drily, 'Yes, I think we'd better forget what it led to. Did you get any orders? I like the sweater, by the way.'

'Thank you. Yes, I got a few. But not as many as I'd hoped. The buyers seemed very wary of trusting me to meet the delivery dates I'd promised. I suppose it's because they haven't dealt with me before,' she conjectured, half to herself. 'Once I fulfil these orders, perhaps they'll be more forthcoming.'

'But they liked your designs?' Casey nodded and he said, 'Well, that's encouraging, surely. Do you knit them all by hand yourself?'

'Oh no, they're mostly done on a machine. But I do have a few hand knitters who work for me.'

Reid's mouth curved into a grin, and all the hardness

in his face suddenly disappeared, giving him a devil-may-care appearance. 'A business tycoon, no less,' he commented mockingly.

Once she had recovered from the effect of that smile, Casey stiffened, sensitive to any condescension. 'I'm merely trying to earn a living as best I can, that's all,' she said shortly.

Immediately his face sobered. 'I beg your pardon. And I commend your enterprise. It's just that you seem so young to be running your own business.'

'I'm not that young. I'm nearly twenty-two. And everyone has to start somewhere.'

'Oh, undoubtedly.' Picking up their empty glasses he said, 'Would you like another?'

'Yes, but could I have something different, please? A shandy or something?'

'Of course. The whisky was just to keep the cold out, was it?'

She smiled and nodded. 'Purely medicinal.'

Reid smiled back, his eyes resting on her face. 'Look, have you eaten yet this evening?'

'Well, no, but I . . .'

'Good,' he interrupted, 'because neither have I, what with one thing and another. I'll see if I can persuade the barmaid to find us something to eat.'

Perhaps the barmaid found him attractive, too, because when he came back with the drinks, he said, 'They'll bring us something in about ten minutes. You were telling me about your business,' he prompted, turning so that he gave her his full attention.

'Was I?' Casey rather doubted that; she didn't usually launch into her life-story with someone she hardly knew.

She shrugged. 'There's nothing much to tell really. I just think up the designs and work them out, then try to sell them.'

'And are you successful?'

'Hardly. At the moment I just about make ends meet, but I only started a few months ago, so hopefully things will improve.' Deciding that she had talked enough about herself, and more than a little curious about her companion, she said, 'How about you? What do you do for a living?'

It was Reid's turn to shrug. 'Oh, I'm in business too. But I can't claim to be an entrepreneur like you. Mine is a family firm, started by my grandfather. We build boats,' he explained.

'Really? I shouldn't have thought there was much call for boats round here.'

'But I don't live here in Westbridge. I live about twenty miles away, near Waterleigh, on the edge of Salford Lake. Do you know it?'

Casey shook her head. 'No, I don't know that side of the county at all, really. And is your business successful, Mr Lomax?' she asked, throwing back at him the question that still rankled.

He laughed. 'Yes, I'm afraid it is. But mine has had over fifty years to establish itself.'

Yes, he would be successful, Casey thought. One look at his well cut clothes and the gold watch on his wrist told you that; and his car, too, had been new and expensive. There was an air of prosperity about him that spelt success and achievement. He was a go-getter, this man, and Casey was convinced that even if he hadn't had his business handed to him on a plate he would have made a success of whatever he had turned his hand to. It was there in the toughness of his jaw, in the energy that emanated from him, and the intelligence that shone from his good eye.

Casey looked away, feeling strangely unsettled, and was glad to see the barmaid coming towards them with a loaded tray. 'Here's our food,' she told him, and moved her glass out of the way so that the girl could put down bowls of steaming hot soup and hunks of crispy French bread with lots of pats of butter. 'Mm, that smells good,' Casey observed, realising just how hungry she was.

Reid looked at her slender, almost boyish figure. 'When did you eat last?'

'Oh, I don't know,' she shrugged. 'I only had time for a cup of coffee at lunch time.'

'And did you eat breakfast this morning?'

'No, there wasn't time. I was working late last night to finish a sample sweater and I overslept.'

'Shall I tell you the one most important thing in running a one-man—or one-woman—business?' Reid asked her, but went on before she could speak. 'It's to realise that your own health is your most important asset. Skipping meals and overworking may seem essential at the time, but it never pays in the long run. New ideas don't come to tired minds, and when you're feeling low you make mistakes which often take twice as much work to put right.' He paused, looking at her, then said, 'I'm sorry. Gratuitous advice from a stranger is probably the last thing you want.'

Casey shook her head. 'Not if it comes from experience. But today is an exception. Usually I eat and sleep properly.'

Again his eye went over her, but he made no comment other than to say, 'Eat your soup.' Which was probably comment enough in itself.

They didn't talk much while they ate the soup, or the fluffy omelettes that followed, but Casey took the opportunity to look around her. She hadn't been in this pub before; it was quite old, with a collection of antique guns fastened to the blackened beams, and lots of plants in gleaming copper and brass holders that caught the flickering light of the fire. There were several other people in the small bar, but it wasn't at all crowded, there were just enough to make it seem convivial and friendly. Casey ate the last scrap of her omelette and sat back in her seat contentedly, thinking that maybe the day hadn't turned out to be so bad, after all.

'Feeling better?' Reid asked her.

'Yes, thank you.' She reached for her bag. 'How much do I owe you for the meal, by the way?'

He made a dismissive gesture. 'Nothing. It's my pleasure.'

'Oh, but I can't let you do that. Especially after all the trouble I've caused you. And besides . . .'

'Yes? Besides what?'

'Well,' Casey said awkwardly. 'I don't really know you.'

His mouth quirking in amusement, Reid said, 'Well, that can soon be remedied. Tell me all about yourself.'

'There's really nothing to tell.'

'Women always say that. Usually it means that they're being modest, or else that they've got something to hide. Which is it with you?'

There was a teasing note in his voice as if he was quite

sure that it was only modesty that held her back, and Casey felt an overpowering urge to come out with something that would really shock him. But maybe he wouldn't be shocked at that; anyone who could sum up a woman's reactions like that must have known a lot of women and be very experienced. Or perhaps it merely meant that he was married. She sneaked a look at his hands, but he wore no ring—not that that meant very much, men didn't have to wear a symbol of bondage as women did, he could be married with half a dozen children. He was certainly old enough to be; Casey judged that he must be in his early thirties, thirty-two or three, she guessed, and suddenly felt an uncharacteristic stab of envy for the unknown woman who was married to so charismatic a man.

Hastily she pulled her thoughts away and said, 'There really isn't. I went to school and then on to art college, and worked for a year in the rag trade before starting up on my own.' She smiled. 'But I hope to improve on that before too long.'

'I'm quite sure you will. As long as you don't have too many days like today.'

'Definitely,' Casey agreed feelingly. 'Look, I really am sorry that I've been such a nuisance to you.' And then, before she could stop herself, added, 'I hope that your wife wasn't keeping dinner for you or anything.'

The mocking line at the corner of Reid's mouth deepened. 'Unfortunately I'm not married so I don't have anyone waiting at home for me. Not even a fiancée, or a steady girlfriend at the moment.' His eye flickered over her. 'How about you?'

'Why no, of course not.' Casey's cheeks started to flush,

'I told you, I live alone.'

'And no fiancé or boyfriend?' She shook her head and he said, 'Well, I'm glad we got that out of the way,' again with that amused smile.

Embarrassed, Casey looked down at her drink. This man was just too astute for comfort. Hurriedly she said, 'I don't know that many people around here. I've been too busy with the business to go out very much.' To her annoyance she heard a defensive note in her voice.

'You should make a point of taking time off. All work and no play, you know.'

Casey sat up straight, suddenly very loath to have him think her dull. Tossing her head, she said, 'Oh, I have loads of friends.'

'I don't doubt it. But presumably you have other hobbies and interests besides your work? Let me see,' he paused, looking at her consideringly. 'I bet you like dancing, going out for meals, the ballet and—going to the theatre,' he hazarded.

Casey's hazel eyes danced with laughter. 'It would be a pretty safe bet. Don't most girls like all those things? But you're wrong about the ballet; I've never been to one so I don't know whether I like it or not. But I love going to the theatre. And to the cinema, when there are any decent films on.' Still somewhat in awe of Reid, she said rather tentatively, 'How about you? What are your interests?'

'I guessed yours. Aren't you going to guess mine?'

The way he looked at her when he said it, and the slightly suggestive note in his voice, almost made Casey say women. With a man her own age, or with someone she knew much better, she probably would have done, facetiously, of course. But with Reid ... He was an entirely different proposition. For one thing he was much older than the usual men she dated, and far more sure of himself. Also there was this undertone of mockery in his manner, as if he didn't take her very seriously—or was it perhaps himself that he didn't take seriously? Whichever it was, Casey found it extremely intriguing. And his air of contained toughness was attractive too, so that she couldn't judge him by comparing him to the men she knew.

Tilting her head to one side, she looked at him pensively, more used now to his injured eye and able to look him in the face. His good eye, she noticed, was dark and flecked like bloodstones, and he had a cleft chin which made her think of the old adage: cleft chin, the devil's within.

'Well?' he asked with mock impatience. 'Surely it can't be all that difficult?'

'But it is. Somehow I can't imagine you doing the things that most men do: playing cricket or golf, going to the pub with your friends, or having lots of business lunches.'

He looked at her with interest. 'No? What, then?'

She shrugged rather helplessly. 'I don't know. I somehow feel that you ought to do something that's exciting, stimulating. Something that takes nerve. Oh dear!' She broke off to laugh. 'I sound like a fortune-teller.'

Reid smiled. 'Maybe you should take it up. That's not at all bad.'

'You do something like that, then?' Casey asked in surprise.

'Something. Oh, I do all the other things as well, like

playing squash—to get fit again after the business lunches—but my main interest is racing.'

'Racing? You mean horses? Or cars?'

Reid shook his dark head. 'Nothing as glamorous as that. I build and race power-boats. Formula One,' he added after a moment's hesitation.

Casey gave him a rather blank look. 'Er—Formula One—should that mean something?'

He gave a rich laugh. 'Obviously not. But don't worry, the world of power-boat racing is a very small and contained one.'

It must be, Casey thought. She could only remember an occasional coverage of races on the television, and then it was only aerial shots of boats racing down the Thames or going round and round a marked course off the coast. As he had said, nowhere near as exciting as horse or car racing, but fascinating enough. And she had been right about him, which pleased her. 'Where do you race?' she asked him. 'On that lake near where you live? Salford Lake, wasn't it?'

'Yes, that's right.' Reid gave her a lazy smile and she had the feeling that he was inwardly amused again. 'I practise there quite a lot, but I have to go away to race.'

'And are you good? Do you win lots of races?'

'My boats are good. I just sit in them and steer.'

Casey very much doubted that and opened her mouth to ask him more about it, but just then the bar door opened and a man came in and called, 'Anyone here order a taxi?' So there was no time to talk further until they had gathered up their belongings and were seated in the back of the taxi, which was just an ordinary car, the driver probably moonlighting to earn some extra money.

'Lucky I'm going in the same direction,' Reid remarked. 'We'll be able to drop you off on the way.' He turned to look at her in the semi-darkness. 'I expect you'll be glad to get home?'

A couple of hours ago Casey would have given a fervent 'yes' to that question, but now she found that she could quite happily have gone on sitting in the pub with Reid, talking, finding out more about him. Only she couldn't tell him that of course, so she just said, 'Yes. Won't you?'

He nodded. 'But you still have the problem of getting your car going tomorrow morning. What will you do?'

'I think I'll have to buy a new battery. That one was pretty useless, anyway. I'll go into Westbridge on the bus and get the garage where I buy the battery from to fix it on for me.' A thought occurred to her and she put a hand to her mouth. 'Oh no, I've just realised; you'll have to take a taxi into Westbridge again tomorrow to collect your car. Oh lord, I'm terribly sor——'

Leaning across, Reid put a finger over her lips. 'It's nothing,' he told her dismissively. 'I can send someone to collect it.'

'But I must at least pay for the taxi,' Casey insisted. 'If it hadn't been for me you wouldn't have needed it.'

'Casey.' Reid's eye held a menacing glint. 'Will you please shut up?'

Realising that she had no choice, Casey said gratefully, 'It's really very kind of you. I don't think many people would have taken it the way you have. Thank you.'

Reid laughed. 'Ah, but then not many damsels in distress are as pretty as you.'

The driver turned round to ask her which was her

house and Casey could have killed him for interrupting something that sounded so promising. 'Oh, it's the fifth one along. The cottage with the thatched roof.' She turned eagerly back to Reid, but he didn't go on and the taxi stopped so she had to say, 'Well, goodnight. And thanks again for—for the meal and everything.'

'It's my pleasure. Goodnight, Casey.'

Getting out of the taxi, she watched as it turned round and lifted a hand to wave as it went past. Then stood and watched its lights fading up the road, wondering why Reid hadn't asked if he could see her again and wishing that he had.

CHAPTER TWO

It was with a sense of regret that she wouldn't be seeing Reid again that Casey set off to walk to the main road to catch the bus into Westbridge the next morning. She was intrigued by him, by his sophistication and obvious experience as much as by his looks, but above all by that occasional glimpse of devil-may-care underneath the sophistication. Like a buccaneer in a business suit, she thought fancifully.

The new battery for the car cost more than she expected, swallowing up all the profit she was likely to make from the orders she had managed to get in London yesterday. This was a blow, but the way her luck was going at the moment it could hardly have been otherwise, she thought gloomily. But at least the garage mechanic agreed to go to the car park and fix the new battery on for her, taking her there with him in his van. Reid's car had already gone, but hers was where they had left it last night, and the car park attendant immediately came over and started going off at her for leaving it across three parking spaces. Stung, Casey retaliated at him for going home without checking that there weren't any cars left.

The silly row strangely made her feel better, and she had to admit that it was great to have a car that started easily again. All she wished now was that Reid would phone her and ask her out. With almost any other man, if she fancied him, Casey would have had no hesitation in

phoning him to say hello, to talk and let him gather that
she was interested. But with Reid she felt strangely
reluctant to do that. After all, he was ten or twelve years
older than she was, and if he had wanted to ask her out he
was quite capable of doing so off his own bat. And yet . . .
Casey remembered how he had told her she was pretty
and had asked whether she had a boyfriend; surely that
meant something. She decided that it did, and drove
home a little faster, eagerly hoping that he would call.

He didn't, of course. Casey waited for a couple of days
and then thought, what the hell! and looked up his
number in the phone book. She couldn't find a private
number for him, but there was a number listed under
Lomax Marine at Waterleigh and she guessed that this
must be his boat-building company. After dialling the
number, her heart beating rather fast, Casey asked for
Reid and was put through to his secretary, a woman with
an attractive voice. 'I'm sorry, Mr Lomax isn't here at the
moment. Can I help you?'

'Er, no, it's a personal call. Will he be back later today
or tomorrow?'

'No, he's abroad at the moment and won't be back
until next week. Can I take a message for him?'

'Well, yes. Perhaps you could tell him that Miss Casey
Everett called?' And she added her phone number.

So that was that. All she could do now was to hope that
he would return her call when he came home. In some
ways it was rather a relief that he hadn't been there; her
only excuse for phoning was to thank him again for
helping her and if he had been busy in the office he might
just have said that's OK, forget it, but now he might
phone when he had time to talk a little more.

Firmly putting Reid out of her mind as much as

possible, Casey concentrated on her work, making sure
that the orders she had got in London were filled quickly
and that the sweaters were absolutely perfect. She just
hoped that the stores would pay for them as quickly;
running your own business, Casey was beginning to find,
was a rather hand-to-mouth existence. Reading her local
paper she noticed that a separates shop was opening
shortly in a nearby town, so she drove over there and had
better luck; the owner gave her an order for three dozen
assorted sweaters.

Perhaps my luck's changing, Casey thought optimistically. Perhaps the orders will start rolling in now. And
perhaps Reid will phone today.

But it was three days later before her doorbell rang one
morning and Casey answered it to find Reid standing on
her doorstep. He was more casually dressed this time, in
cord trousers and a zip-up jacket, the eye-patch giving
him a rakish air. He smiled. 'Hello.'

'Why—hello! Come in.' Casey stood back to let him
enter, acutely conscious that she was wearing her
working clothes of very faded jeans and baggy sweater,
the sleeves pushed up to her elbows. 'In here.' She led him
into her small but pleasant sitting-room.

He looked round, liking what he saw, and then turned
to her. And some feminine instinct told Casey that he
liked what he saw there, too. 'Did you manage to get your
car fixed?' he asked.

'Yes, thanks. The garage put a new battery on for me
and it's been fine since then.' She realised that he was
probably going to ask her why she had phoned, so to
forestall him Casey said quickly, 'Would you like a
coffee?'

'That would be nice. But if I'm interrupting your work . . .'

'Oh, no. It's no trouble. I was about to have one myself. It won't take a minute.'

She went out to the kitchen and Reid followed her there, leaning against the door-jamb to watch her. 'The front of your cottage reminds me of a tea-cosy,' he remarked. 'With its red brick and thatched roof.'

Casey laughed. 'That's what I thought the first time I saw it. So I planted some roses on either side of the door to complete the picture.'

She finished making the coffees and picked up the tray to carry it into the sitting-room, but Reid took it from her.

'I'll light the fire.' She put a match to the already laid fire, the wood soon catching and giving a warm, crackling glow to the room.

'How's the sweater business going?' Reid asked lazily.

Picking up her mug of coffee, Casey sat in the armchair opposite his, on the other side of the fire. 'Not too badly. I got another order last week.' As she looked across at him it occurred to her that it was almost like being married, sitting on either side of the fire like this.

'Do you only sell to shops? I wondered if I might buy one from you.'

Her cosy fantasy bursting like a pricked balloon, Casey said stiffly, 'Why yes, of course. I'm afraid they're rather expensive, but I could give you a special price.'

Her change to a businesslike tone brought a flash of amusement to Reid's eyes. 'Thank you, that's very good of you.'

'Not at all. I'm really very grateful to you for helping me out on the night we met. That's what I phoned to tell you, by the way,' she finished rather lamely.

With a grin, Reid said, 'I could cheerfully have murdered you when I got to the car park and found your car right behind mine. If you'd been a man ...'

'You would have expressed your feelings rather more forcefully, I take it?' Casey interrupted.

'And some. In fact, I was rather disappointed when you turned out to be a girl. I wasn't able to give full vent to my feelings.'

'You were pretty mad, anyway,' Casey pointed out, remembering.

'Was I? I apologise.'

'No, you had a right to be angry. But I thought you really were going to murder me when you found that we were locked in.'

'Mm. But that turned out to be an advantage rather than a calamity. If we hadn't been locked in I would just have driven off and I'd never have got to know you.' He paused while Casey, her heart beating, waited eagerly for him to go on. 'And I would never have been able to come and buy a sweater from you.'

Her face tightened as Casey tried hard not to show her disappointment. She opened her mouth to agree with him, but Reid added, 'For my sister—for her birthday.'

'Your—sister?'

'Yes.'

'Oh! I—I see.'

Their eyes met and it was all there in that one glance; the acknowledgement of the primeval instincts that had made them sexually aware of each other, and the knowledge that they were about to embark on a relationship which might only lead to friendship, but which *could* develop into much, much more.

It was Casey who looked away first, her cheeks flushed,

lips parted as if she was a little breathless. 'Do you know what size your sister is?'

'About a fourteen, I should think.'

So he knew enough about women to guess their size, did he? Somehow that was a personal thing now, almost a challenge.

'Your—secretary, was it?—said that you were abroad somewhere last week. Was it business or a holiday?'

He gave a twisted kind of smile. 'Hardly a holiday, but not strictly business. I was taking part in a race and managed to get orders for a few boats while I was there. In Munich.'

'Munich? I didn't realise that you went abroad to race.'

Again that amused look, but almost as if he was laughing at himself. 'I suppose you just thought that I went round and round the lake? No, it's a little more than that.' Finishing his coffee, he said, 'Where do you work?'

'There's a room at the back. Perhaps you'd—like to see?'

'Very much.' Reid stood up. 'Then I'll be able to choose that sweater.'

They went into the extended back room of the cottage where Casey had her three knitting-machines, and a large drawing-board where she sat and worked out her designs. She was in the process of working on one at the moment and Reid asked her several questions about it, surprising her by how quickly he understood. 'Why three machines?' he asked her. 'You can only work on one at a time, surely?'

'Yes, but the machines do different things, and quite often when I'm trying out a design I might try different ways of doing it. Also if I'm working on a garment and I get an idea for something else I can try it out on another machine.'

Reid nodded approvingly. 'It's always a good idea to try and develop a new idea as soon as you think of it, otherwise you often tend to lose it again. How many different designs do you have?'

'About ten basic designs, but I do variations on them, vary the colours and textures of the wool, or put different belts or buttons on them, so that it actually appears as if there's a much wider range. I like women to feel that they're wearing something that's individual, that they won't go out and run the risk of seeing one exactly the same.' She took out some sweaters to demonstrate what she meant and Reid moved closer to her to look. Casey went on explaining how she worked, but she was very conscious of his closeness, of his height and bulk, and the sheer masculinity of him.

He asked questions, too. Pertinent questions, not just the usual commonplace ones. And because Reid showed an intelligent interest, Casey was soon talking animatedly, her hazel eyes sparkling with enthusiasm, her cheeks a little flushed. Once she turned to Reid as she showed him a sweater, but found him looking at her instead, an absorbed expression on his face. Her voice dying in her throat, Casey gazed up at him. Slowly Reid reached out and put a hand on her shoulder. Her heart beating, Casey waited for him to kiss her, but his hand merely tightened a moment before he carried on with the conversation. Struggling to hide an intense feeling of disappointment, she answered him as best she could, but the animation in her face had died a little.

Reid chose a sweater for his sister, one with little pearl buttons on the sleeves, in a soft blue that he said would match his sister's eyes. And he paid for it there and then, in cash, too, which was very useful. He moved towards the door, but Casey, not wanting him to go, had an inspiration and said, 'Shall I gift-wrap it for you?'

'Could you? That would be great. I'm afraid I'm all thumbs when it comes to that kind of thing.'

'Of course. I know I've got some pretty paper somewhere.' Leading the way back into the sitting-room, Casey took the paper from an old bow-fronted chest of drawers and knelt on the floor to wrap it for him and add a bow of silk ribbon. 'There. Will that be OK?'

'It will be fine.' Reaching down a hand, Reid helped her to her feet, slowly drawing her up beside him. He gazed intently into her face, desire sharpening his features, then gave a small exclamation and pulled her almost roughly into his arms to kiss her.

From the moment his lips touched hers it felt right. And sensuous. And exhilarating. There was no thought of resistance as Casey put her arms round his neck, returning his kiss avidly, her mouth opening as soon as he demanded it until she felt as if she were being carried along on a long, delicious tidal wave of sensuality. Reid's hands moved down her back to her waist, holding her against him as his tongue hungrily explored the soft recesses of her mouth, his eagerness awakening a sharp awareness deep inside her.

He was very experienced. Although he kissed her so demandingly, he did so with the knowledge that could come only from experience, his lips, his tongue, teasing and titillating, one moment giving, the next taking, and savouring her response. And Casey had never before given herself so overwhelmingly to a man, without any reserve, only living for the moment and never wanting it to end.

So it was Reid who at length drew back, his breathing a little uneven, his one eye glittering down at her. 'Well, well, well,' he said on a dawning note of realisation that was almost a sigh.

Her cheeks flushed, Casey said, 'What does that mean?'

Reid gave a small laugh. 'It means a hell of a lot of things, but mostly that I got a lot more than I bargained for.' Feeling that she had been too responsive, Casey began to draw away, but he held her still, saying reassuringly, 'Which I'm very happy to admit.'

'And what else?'

Bringing up a finger he tapped her gently on the nose. 'Maybe I'll tell you some other time.' He smiled down at her. 'Now, what was that list of things you liked? Eating out, dancing, the theatre and the cinema, wasn't that it? Well, why don't we work our way through the list, and start by going out to dinner? Can you make tomorrow night?' And when Casey nodded, her face glowing, he went on, 'OK, I'll pick you up at seven.'

He left then, but Casey was far too excited to settle back to her work. She kept breaking off to gaze dreamily into space, working out what she would wear tomorrow, wondering where Reid would take her, but most of all remembering how exciting it had been to be held in his arms, and how she could have gone on kissing him for ever, a feeling so new that she was almost afraid to dwell on it.

Casey thought of Reid often during the rest of that day and the next, and by seven was ready and waiting, her hair newly washed, and wearing a red and white print

dress that she knew suited her. It was just as well she was
ready, because Reid was almost ten minutes early. She
opened the door to him and he walked straight into her
tiny hall, took her in his arms and kissed her so hard that
Casey had to renew her lipstick before they could go out.
'I missed you,' he said softly, his fingers running down
her cheek.

'But you only saw me yesterday.'

'It seems like a week.'

Which was extremely flattering to Casey's ego and set
the tune for the whole of that wonderful evening, and all
the times he took her out over the next few weeks. As he
had promised, Reid took her to all the places she liked:
restaurants, the cinema, to a dinner and dance, and once
up to London for the theatre and a meal afterwards. Just
to be with him was heady enough, but Casey liked it best
when he took her dancing. He was a good dancer and
could do the traditional ballroom dances like quicksteps
and foxtrots as well as the modern stuff. Which was fun,
but nowhere near as good as when the band played slow
numbers and he held her close while they danced, their
bodies often touching, their heads just a kiss away, her
hand tightly held in his. So satisfying and yet so
tantalising at the same time.

Casey noticed that people often turned to look at them,
some of the women's glances openly admiring Reid, and
always with that touch of curiosity because of his bad eye,
which gave him such a rakish air. But he would have
attracted women's glances anyway, Casey guessed,
because he was so tall and good-looking. She was still a
little in awe of him, although that lessened every time
they went out together, but she hadn't yet summoned up
the courage to ask him about his eye, how he had hurt it.

He never mentioned it himself, and she was afraid that he might be sensitive about it, although it certainly didn't stop him from doing anything; he was an extremely good driver, the patch in no way impairing his ability.

There was something slightly enigmatic about him, too. Although he was easy and relaxed enough most of the time, she would sometimes catch him unawares and surprise a closed expression on his face, and feel that part of him was hidden from her, that there were forces inside him that he concealed from the rest of the world.

He kissed her often during those weeks, before he had to go abroad again, his kisses lifting her into a temporary state of blissful pleasure, but awakening a growing need, a longing for fulfilment that kisses couldn't satisy. But Reid didn't do more than kiss and caress her whenever he came into the cottage to say goodnight. Sometimes he didn't even come in, but merely kissed her goodbye in the car and then walked her to her gate. But in some ways this added to the excitement of going out with him, this feeling that he was the master of the situation and in control of it, that he wouldn't go further until he felt it right and not before. And the knowledge that when he did it would be all the more wonderful for having waited.

While Reid was away, in Stockholm this time, Casey paid a belated visit to her family home. Her parents lived in Norfolk, in a house not far from the east coast, a flat area of land that was pleasant in summer but where the wind blew coldly off the sea during winter, so that the region was less populated than most of England; a fact that had forced Casey to move away to the more populated south to find outlets for her work. Casey went up there for the weekend, and at dinner that evening sat down with her parents and her younger brother, Mark, and told them all about the ups and downs of her business life.

'And I've had orders for another fifty sweaters from one of the London stores I went to,' she told them happily. 'It seems that they sold out of the half-dozen that they originally ordered within two days.'

'That *is* good,' her mother agreed. 'You'll be another Laura Ashley before you're finished.' She looked at her daughter shrewdly. 'And you seem very happy; you've got more colour in your cheeks than you had. Are you getting out a bit more? Not concentrating on work all the time.'

'No, I've been going out a lot. I went up to London to the theatre last week.'

Mark laughed. 'Spending all your profits, eh?'

'Why no, I . . .' Casey paused, then said, 'No, it was a date. Someone took me.'

Her mother's ears pricked up. 'Oh? A local boy?'

'Yes, he's quite local,' Casey admitted, but chuckled inwardly; anyone less like a boy than Reid would be hard to find.

'What's he like?' Mrs Everett demanded. 'What does he do? Are you serious about him?'

'Oh, Mum! I've only been going out with him for about six weeks. He—er—helped me when my car broke down, and I've been out with him a few times since.'

'You should have brought him up with you.'

'I couldn't; he's abroad on business and won't be back for a while.'

'Goes abroad a lot, does he?' her father put in.

'Quite a bit. As a matter of fact he has his own business; he builds boats. And he has to go abroad to get orders for them,' she admitted, not without a slight note of pride. Adding, 'Oh, and he does some power-boat racing as well.'

'Really?' Mark looked at her with interest. 'I've started to take part in that myself. I go over to Yarmouth to the Power-Boat Club and take part in two-man or three-man races whenever I can. It's really great. But expensive, though. What's your boyfriend's name?'

'It's Lomax. Reid Lomax. He told me he takes part in something called Formula One.'

Mark had just taken a mouthful of food when she spoke and he choked as he swallowed in surprise and it went down the wrong way. 'Something called Formula One!' he spluttered as soon as he could speak. 'My God, Casey, don't you even know who Reid Lomax *is*?'

'What do you mean? Have you heard of him, then?'

'Heard of him? Everyone who's had anything at all to do with power-boats has heard of him. Look, simpleton, Formula One power-boat racing is like Formula One Grand Prix racing. The drivers mostly drive team-sponsored boats and they travel all over the world on the Grand Prix circuit. The racing that I do is a world away from what Reid Lomax does. It's like—it's like comparing a local car rally to a World Championship Grand Prix race. *Now* do you understand?'

Casey stared at him. 'Yes, I suppose so. And is Reid good?'

'Good?' Mark looked at her pityingly. 'My dear girl, your boyfriend just happens to have been the world champion twice before and is in the lead for this year's World Championship, that's all. And he probably would have been the champion last year if he hadn't had a bad accident that kept him out of a couple of races.' He stared at her as a thought occurred to him. 'But one of the things that's best known about Lomax is that he designs and builds his own boats. He doesn't even have a sponsor. Everyone says that he's absolutely loaded.'

Casey gulped, overwhelmed by what she had heard. 'You—you mean he's rich?' she asked unbelievingly.

'He must be if he can afford to run his own boats. Of course, every time he wins a race it means marvellous publicity for his company,' Mark told her, pleased to be able to air his knowledge.

'And do you think that's why he does it—to publicise the boats?' Casey asked, still trying to sort out the impressions the news had made on her mind.

'Of course not. I told you, Casey, he's really good. Drivers who are that good have to be entirely dedicated and professional. Besides, if he'd only been in it for the publicity he would never have gone back to driving after that crash he had last year.'

'Seems you've found yourself quite a celebrity,' her father remarked, his eyes on her slightly troubled face. 'Perhaps you'd better find out more about him.'

Casey gave a light laugh. 'As I told you, I've only known him a short while. He's abroad again at the moment and he might not even ask me to go out with him again when he gets back.' Quickly she changed the subject, asking about some of her old school friends, but when she at last escaped to her room that night after what had seemed like a never-ending evening, her thoughts were full of all that she had heard. So Reid was rich, was he? This wasn't really anything new now she came to think about it; he had always seemed to take money for granted and had been more than generous whenever he had taken her out. But there was a difference between having enough money and being rich. Wealth was something that was outside Casey's experience; her father was an accountant and although they had never really wanted for anything, it had been taken for granted that she and Mark had to take holiday jobs and work their way through college. And she had had to save up the money to rent her cottage and pay for the knitting-machines to start up her business, although her parents had helped her all they could.

Putting the idea of Reid being wealthy out of her mind, Casey's thoughts turned to his racing, and the accident that her brother had told her about. Was that, she wondered, where Reid had hurt his eye? She presumed that the accident had happened during a race, although Mark hadn't definitely said so. Was it dangerous, then? Grand Prix motor racing certainly was; you were always hearing about crashes and drivers being injured. Casey turned uneasily, wondering just how badly Reid had been hurt. Not badly enough to put him off, obviously. But it was also evident that her conception of him racing round and round the local lake merely to advertise his boats had been entirely wrong. Casey lay gazing into the darkness, remembering the scenes she had seen on television and at the cinema of beautiful girls standing in the pits clocking up the times of their racing-driver husbands or boyfriends. Did power-boat drivers' girls do that? she wondered, picturing herself in the role and rather liking it. The after-race parties would probably be fun, too. And it all sounded glamorous and exciting. Her mind dwelt on this for a while, her mouth curved into a smile as she imagined herself with Reid, but then her eyes shadowed again as she remembered his accident. First thing tomorrow, Casey decided, she must get Mark on his own and make him tell her as much as he knew about it.

But her brother went out early the next morning, so it
wasn't until after lunch that she managed to think up an
excuse and the two of them were able to leave the house
to walk to a garden centre about a mile away, ostensibly
to buy some plants for their mother.

'OK,' Mark said resignedly. 'You must want something. You don't usually want my company when you go
for a walk. But make it quick; I've got a video film I want
to watch this afternoon.'

'Oh, honestly, how do you expect to get anywhere
when you spend all your time watching the television?'
Casey admonished him.

'Don't you start; I have enough with Mum. I suppose
you want to ask me about your friend Reid Lomax.'

'Yes.' Casey stopped and turned to look at him. 'About
his accident.'

Mark looked surprised. 'I would have thought you'd
be more interested in his business and his racing history.'

'I am. But first I'd like to know how his accident
happened. It was in a race, I take it?'

'Well, no, I don't think it was actually. I seem to
remember it was during a practice session. His boat took
off and rolled over or something.'

'What do you mean—took off?'

'Well, the boats are so light and the engines that they
use so powerful, that sometimes the boats just start to take
off, like an aeroplane.' He gestured with his hand. 'But,
not having any wings, they just roll over and the driver
gets thrown out.'

'But how can he get hurt if he just goes into the water?'
Casey objected.

'Didn't they teach you anything at school?' Mark

demanded in brotherly long-suffering. 'The boats are
going so fast that when the driver hits the water it's like
hitting a block of cement. They literally bounce against
the surface until they slow down enough to go in. I
haven't seen it happen myself, but I've seen it on
television and it's quite spectacular.'

'Bloodthirsty little devil! And you say this happened to
Reid? Do you know how badly he was hurt?'

'Not offhand. But I'm pretty sure I read an article
about it in one of my copies of *Power-Boating* magazine. I
take it every month and share it with some of the others
in the Club.'

Casey began to walk on again, but after a moment
said, 'I'd like to read it when we get back home.'

'Sorry.' Mark shook his head. 'I'll have passed it on to
someone else. But I can find it and send it to you, if you
like?' When Casey nodded, he went on, 'Actually I could
probably bring it down to you. And perhaps in return
you could introduce me to your boyfriend. Perhaps he
might give me a few tips on boat-handling. He might
even let me have a go in one of his boats,' he added
optimistically.

'Don't you dare!' Casey exclaimed. 'I don't want
you interfering before I've even ...' She stopped
precipitately.

'Before what?' Mark demanded, enjoying teasing her.
'Before you've got him really hooked?'

For a moment Casey's eyes were troubled. 'No, not so
much that. Before I've made up my own mind about
him.'

But if Casey had had any doubts about him they were
almost instantly dispelled when Reid appeared unexpectedly on her doorstep early in the evening a couple of

weeks later, his arms so full of flowers and parcels that he couldn't get hold of her to kiss her.

'Reid!' Casey exclaimed in delighted surprise. 'When did you get back? I thought you weren't due until Saturday.'

'I managed to get back a day early. Here, help me put these on the table,' he instructed as he followed her into the sitting-room. His arms empty, he turned to her impatiently. 'For God's sake, come here, woman. If I have to wait another minute to kiss you I shall go mad.' Pulling her into his arms, he looked down at her face for a minute before bending his head to kiss her, a kiss that more than proved that he had missed her while he had been away. Not until they were both breathless did they break apart, but Reid still held her in his arms, his face nuzzling her neck, so close that she could hear his heart beating. 'Missed me?' he murmured.

Casey lifted her head to look at him, her emotions mirrored in her eyes. 'Yes,' she admitted sincerely. 'I did miss you.'

Putting his hands on either side of her head, Reid kissed her again, long and lingeringly, then grinned and said, 'Look at what I've brought you back.'

And in the next few minutes Casey began to find out what it was like to have a rich man for a boyfriend. Not only had he brought her flowers, but also some French perfume, a beautiful silver bracelet, some embroidered handkerchiefs, and a big box of chocolates.

'Reid!' Casey sat on the floor and looked at all the things spread around her. 'It's like Christmas!'

'Wrong season. With summer in mind I also bought you this.' With a rather devilish grin, he handed her yet another parcel.

Casey gave him a wary look, beginning to recognise that gleam in his eye. Opening the parcel, she found a beautifully worked, but very brief, crocheted bikini. 'Wow!' She held the pieces up. 'There isn't exactly a lot of it is there?' She gave him an impish look. 'And do you really think that our English summer is going to be hot enough for me to wear it?'

Smiling in return, Reid answered, 'Who knows, maybe you'll go on holiday somewhere much warmer.'

As Casey hadn't mentioned a holiday and certainly couldn't afford to go abroad, that could be taken as a loaded remark, but she wisely didn't pursue it, instead saying, 'Tell me all about your trip. Did you take part in another race? And did you win?'

'Yes, I took part in another race, and yes, luckily, I won. Which is good for business.'

'Is that why you do it?' Casey asked curiously, but trying to keep her voice light. 'Just to sell boats?'

'No, I enjoy it too. It's a sport that's been bred into me almost. My father used to race too, and he started me off when I was quite young. But how about you? What have you been doing while I've been away? Lots more orders coming in?'

'Yes, I've been really busy.' Happily she told him all about it.

'Good. Well done. And I'm glad you've been kept busy. I wouldn't like to think that you had time enough to go out with other men. Did you?'

His voice had grown serious and to Casey's surprise and gratification she recognised a note of jealousy in his question. Getting to her feet, she went across to him and let him pull her on to his lap. 'No, I didn't go out with anyone else. Although . . .'

Reid's hand tightened on hers. 'Yes?'

'Although I did go home to see my family.'

'Tease,' he told her with a grin. 'Where would you like to go tonight?'

She put a hand up to touch his face. 'Somewhere quiet,' she said softly. 'Somewhere where we can talk and no one will notice us. Where we can eat by the light of candles and take our time over our meal. Where we can dance if we want to or just sit and relax and talk.'

'Mmm, sounds heaven,' Reid agreed. 'But where is there around here where we can do all those things?'

Casey smiled up at him. 'Can't you guess? Why, here, of course!'

'Here?' Reid looked into her face, a warm flame deep in his eyes. 'Are you sure you wouldn't rather go out?'

'No. That's if you . . .'

Putting a finger over her lips, Reid said, 'I would much rather stay here. Thank you.' And he replaced his finger with his lips. 'I thought of you a lot while I was away.'

'Did you? What about me?'

'That I wished we were together. That I would like to have taken you with me and shown you Stockholm.' As he spoke they exchanged small kisses and Reid's arms tightened round her. 'Oh, Casey, Casey. It's good to be back and hold you in my arms again.' He smiled at her. 'I think you've bewitched me. Usually I enjoy going away to race, but this time I just longed to be back home.'

They kissed again until Casey rather breathlessly pushed him away. 'Hey! If I'm going to cook dinner for us . . .'

Reid held up his hands. 'I know, I know. Want some help?'

'Can you cook?'

'No, but I'm very good at stirring things.'

Laughing, Casey got to her feet and looked down at him, but then her face grew intent as she said softly, 'I'm very glad you're back, too.' And gave him an impulsive hug before hurrying into the kitchen.

Reid's idea of helping was mostly to stand around drinking sherry and talk while he watched her, but when everything was simmering nicely he went out to get a bottle of wine, giving Casey the opportunity to change into a long black skirt and white silk shirt with a tucked bodice, to pin up her hair and put on some make-up.

Reid whistled appreciatively when he came back and saw her. 'You look stunning.'

He went to kiss her, but she pushed him away. 'No, I must see to the meal.'

'Tyrant,' Reid complained. 'Am I always going to have this trouble with you?'

Casey's heart skipped a beat, but she answered with mock severity, 'Certainly. I never allow that kind of thing in the kitchen.'

'What kind of thing?'

'You know very well what I mean.'

'This, presumably.' And coming up behind her, Reid began to kiss the back of her neck. 'I like your hair up like that. It reveals bits of you I haven't seen before. And very kissable they are too.'

Squirming deliciously, Casey pulled away, then picked up a spoon and rapped him on the knuckles with it. **'Go and wait in the dining-room or this meal will** never get finished,' she ordered sternly.

Reid's good eye laughed down at her, and it occurred to Casey that he looked very happy, but then she felt very happy too. He went away, enabling her to finish cooking the meal, and soon they were sitting opposite each other, the curtains drawn, the candles lit and the fire crackling in the old hearth of the inglenook. Reid had put on a tape of love songs that played softly in the background, and the bottle of wine turned out to be champagne.

'We ought to drink to something,' Casey suggested when Reid had filled her glass. 'What shall it be?'

Picking up his own glass Reid clinked it against hers. 'There's really only one toast to make, isn't there?' he said, looking intently into her eyes. 'To us—and to our future.'

And as Casey slowly nodded and drank the toast she was suddenly and completely certain that her future did indeed lie with Reid, that she loved him and wanted to spend the rest of her life with him.

CHAPTER THREE

AFTER they had drunk the toast, Reid covered her hand with his for a moment, but then, rather to Casey's relief, began to talk of other things. She answered him, but was in the grip of such deep emotion that at first she couldn't concentrate. It was only when they were eating their pudding that she was able to join in the conversation properly again and say, 'My brother was very impressed when I told him that I'd met you. I had no idea that you were so famous. It seems that he's into power-boat racing himself. He immediately demanded to meet you so that he could pick your brain.'

'How old is he?' Reid asked.

'Just twenty.'

'Ah, just the age to be full of enthusiasm.' He looked at her shrewdly. 'And I suppose he'd like me to give him a ride in one of my boats?'

'Well, yes, he would,' Casey admitted reluctantly. 'But of course you don't have to . . .'

Lifting his hand in a silencing gesture, Reid said, 'It's all right. I don't mind. He might be good. And as it happens I'm looking for someone to train to take over my back-up boat.' He sat back in his chair and smiled at her. 'And anyway, isn't it about time that you took me to meet your family?'

Casey's heart skipped another beat and it was almost a minute before she could say, 'All right. Perhaps we could go up there one Sunday.'

Leaning forward Reid picked up her hand and played with her fingers, twining them within his own and bending to kiss them. '*Next* Sunday,' he said firmly. Then he raised his eyebrows and looked directly into her eyes. 'Yes?'

A simple question, but Casey realised that it meant so much more. 'Yes,' she answered without hesitation. 'We'll go next Sunday.'

Reid gave a small smile, his hand tightening on hers until it hurt. 'Good,' he said on a soft note of satisfaction and happiness.

They drank their coffee sitting by the fire; Reid in the armchair and Casey sitting on the floor at his feet. They didn't talk much, but Reid occasionally put his hand down to stroke her hair or run a finger down the length of her neck. Lifting her head to look at him, Casey felt so happy that she thought her heart would burst with it, as if her chest was too small to contain a heart that was so swollen with happiness. How strange, she thought. How strange that we should have met like we did—and that we both feel like this, when ordinarily we wouldn't have met at all.

Tentatively she lifted her hand and put it on Reid's knee. Immediately he put his over it and pulled her up on to his lap. His eyes darkening with desire, he bent to kiss her, savouring her lips, tasting their sweetness. Taking the pins from her hair, he ran his fingers through its silken tresses, taking pleasure in its softness. His lips moved to her throat, delightfully insinuating and yet tantalising too, awakening the now familiar ache of need deep in her stomach, that seemed to grow until every part of her body wanted to be touched, to be kissed.

Casey's lips parted on a little moan of pleasure. 'Oh, Reid.'

'I know, sweetheart,' he murmured back. 'Believe me, I know.' His mouth found hers again, kissing her with ever-deepening passion. His hand went to the tiny buttons on her shirt, slowly undoing them. Casey wished fervently that she hadn't worn that blouse, there were so many buttons and he was taking so long when her body was so hungry for his touch. At last it was undone and Reid pushed the soft material aside to kiss along the line of her shoulder, to linger at the hollow of her shoulderblade. He took off her blouse, then reached behind her to undo her bra and slowly, infinitely slowly, take it off. He let his eyes drink their fill of her small breasts, softly rounded but with the firmness of youth, the tiny nipples like the unopened buds of pale pink roses. Gently he lifted his hand to touch them, his lips parted in concentration. It was the first time he had ever done so, the first time he had ever done more than kiss her. And Casey knew that it was because she was special, that he had held back because he wanted her to be sure, so that what happened between them now would be a wonderful experience that they would always remember, and not just a commonplace coupling between two people who fancied each other.

He explored her gently but knowledgeably, his fingers rousing her libido so that her nipples hardened with desire, buds waiting to open. And only then did Reid bend to take one in his mouth, softly sucking and pulling, while his hand gently fondled the other.

Her heart pounding, Casey trembled as she lay in his arms, loving what Reid was doing to her, but the urgent need it aroused in her was almost more than she could bear. Putting her hands on his shoulders, she pushed him away so that he lifted his head to look at her. 'Reid.' She said his name so softly it was only a breath, but then suddenly kissed him fiercely on the mouth, her hands digging into him with an urgency that overwhelmed her. 'Reid,' she said again, her voice rising almost on a note of pleading. 'Hold me. Please hold me.'

He did so, feeling the wild beating of her heart against his chest. After a few moments, his mouth against the hair covering her ear, Reid said, 'Casey, my darling. I want you very much but . . .'

'And I want you.' She turned her head quickly to look at him, their faces only inches apart. 'I—I love you, Reid.'

'Oh, my darling girl.' He kissed her deeply, tenderly. 'And I you. So much. So much.' For a moment Reid just held her in his arms, but then he tilted her face to look at him. 'Casey, you're probably going to think this is absolutely crazy, but—well, I've had women before. Quite a few in fact, over the years. But I've always hoped that one day I would fall in love with someone like you. Someone very special. So, darling, much as I want you, we will only ever get married once and I would very much like to do it properly.'

Casey looked at him mistily, her throat dry. 'Have—have a white wedding, you mean?'

'Yes, of course. And as soon as possible. But not only that. I'd like our wedding night to be our first night together.' He gave her a rather rueful look. 'I suppose you think that that's a completely archaic attitude.'

'No, I don't.' Casey shook her head, silly tears of happiness in her eyes. 'I think it's wonderful,' she said chokily. 'But—well, do you really think we could last out that long?'

Reid gave a burst of laughter and hugged her. 'It won't be easy, especially when you're lovely enough to drive a man crazy. But the racing season is really getting under way now and I shall be away quite a lot, so maybe we'll manage.'

Lying back in his arms, Casey lifted a finger to trace the outline of his profile, her eyes on his face, thinking about his injured eye and the accident that she was sure must have caused it.

As if reading her mind Reid said on a harsh note, 'Do you mind? About my eye?'

'Of course not. Oh no, Reid, don't ever think that.' Leaning forward, Casey gently kissed the eye-patch to reassure him, to prove that it didn't repel her at all. She would have liked to ask him, then, what had happened, but didn't want to spoil so wonderful an evening, so instead she gave a little smile. 'As a matter of fact I find it rather attractive. The first time I saw you I thought you looked like a pirate. I also thought you were quite fascinating.'

'Did you now? But not half as fascinating as I find you, my darling, beautiful girl.' And Reid bent to kiss and caress her again, so that words became superfluous when they could so much better *show* each other how they felt.

They didn't say anything to her family when they went up to Norfolk on the following Sunday, but it must have been pretty obvious from the way they looked at each other that they were very much in love. Her parents were a little taken aback at first to find that Reid was a man of thirty-three rather than the boy they had expected, but they very soon fell under his spell, her mother especially.

Mark, of course, would have monopolised Reid for the whole day if he had been allowed to. As it was he asked him endless questions which Reid answered with good-humoured patience, and he even seemed to be pleased by Mark's keenness, offering him his coveted ride in one of his racing power-boats.

After lunch they all drove over to the coast and walked along the beach, its smooth sands stretching for miles, the sea sparkling in the spring sunshine. Sometimes they walked as a group, sometimes splitting up into twos or threes, but it was some time before Casey could prise Mark away from Reid long enough to hiss, 'Did you find that article?' at him.

Mark looked surprised. 'Do you still want it?'

'Yes. Have you got it yet?'

He nodded. 'I was going to bring it down to you, but then Mum said you were coming today so I didn't bother. It's up in my room.' He looked at her curiously. 'Haven't you asked Reid about it yet, then? I should have thought you would have, now you've gone this far.'

'What's that supposed to mean?' Casey demanded.

'Well, bringing him home to meet Mum and Dad and all that,' Mark explained with a grin. 'You've never brought anyone home before. Not like this, making a special trip. And anyway, it's pretty obvious that you're gone on each other.'

'Well, maybe we are,' Casey admitted. 'But don't say anything to Mum and Dad yet.'

Mark gave a snort of laughter. 'As if I need to. They've got eyes too, you know.'

Casey smiled softly. 'Yes, I suppose so. But I still want

to read that article, so slip it to me when Reid isn't around, will you?'

'OK. But why don't you just come right out and ask him yourself?'

'I don't know. He never talks about it. I think I'd like to know what happened before I decide,' Casey explained, her eyes a little troubled. 'I don't want to remind him of something he might be trying hard to forget.'

So before they left Mark waited until Reid was saying goodbye to their mother and passed her a folded sheet of paper which Casey quickly put into her bag.

They waved as they drove away until her parents were out of sight and then Reid gave a 'Phew' of relief and pretended to wipe sweat from his brow. 'Thank goodness we got through that ordeal OK.'

Casey gave a delighted laugh. 'Don't tell me you were nervous! I don't *believe* it.'

'Of course I was nervous. Meeting one's future in-laws for the first time can be a nerve-racking experience for a man. I was scared stiff.'

'Rubbish. I can't imagine you ever being afraid of anything.'

They had come to a red set of traffic lights and Reid turned to her as they waited. 'You couldn't be more wrong. There's one thing I'm completely terrified of.'

'Oh? What's that?' Casey asked in surprise, all sorts of thoughts running through her mind.

Reaching across, Reid covered her hand with his as it lay in her lap. 'Of losing you, of course,' he said with deep sincerity. 'That I couldn't bear.' His eyes held hers for a long moment, but then a car behind them hooted impatiently and he turned away to concentrate on the road.

It was almost midnight before Reid left her and Casey had the opportunity to take the article from her bag and read it. Strangely, she felt almost reluctant to do so, as if she was prying into something secret. But that was silly; the article was public property, there to be read by anyone who had bought the magazine.

There was no date on the page, merely a description of a Formula One race that had taken place in Milan. It began with a headline saying, 'World Championship hopes dashed for Reid Lomax', and went on to give an account of his crash, which had happened much as Mark had said; the boat taking off and rolling over. Reid, it stated, had been taken to hospital unconscious, suffering from head injuries and severe concussion. It had been feared at first that he had brain damage, but (at the time) he was on his way to making a good recovery, although the doctors didn't hold out much hope of saving the sight of his right eye.

Casey put down the cutting, feeling physically sick, but this was suddenly replaced by fierce anger. 'How dare he risk his life like that? How dare he?' She thrust the cutting away in her handbag, unable even to look at it again, but determined that she would ask Reid about it the next time she saw him. If she was going to marry him then she had the right to know.

But although Reid rang her every day, he was busy and wasn't able to see her again until a few days later, by which time the first shock of reading the article had worn off a little. It seemed ages since she had seen him so that Casey ran eagerly to open the door when he arrived. Reid stepped inside, took her in his arms and kissed her hungrily, having missed her as much as she'd missed him. His kiss, of course, drove everything else out of her mind, and it was quite some time before Reid even bothered to close the door.

He laughed softly as he held her. 'I think we'd better set the date for our wedding pretty soon, don't you? How about June?'

'June sounds wonderful,' Casey agreed, kissing his neck. 'But it's almost two months away.'

She felt a tremor run through him as she bit his earlobe. 'We could always make it early June.' Her tongue teased him and he shuddered, his arms tightening around her.

'*Very* early June,' he amended. 'You minx! I can't stand that. Come here.'

But Casey teasingly eluded him and ran into the sitting-room, dodging round the furniture until Reid caught her. She shrieked when he grabbed her from behind, half lifting her off her feet as she struggled to get away, but his arms tightened and for the first time she felt his immense, contained strength.

Laughing, Reid put his hand over her mouth. 'Quiet, woman. Or else the neighbours will think I'm raping you.' Turning her round, he held her against him, his eye glittering down into hers. It was only a game, and one that she had started herself, but to have him chase her like that gave Casey a delicious thrill of danger and excitement. For a moment Reid had again been the pirate and she his unwilling captive. But there was nothing at all unwilling in the way she responded when he kissed her again, pressing herself against him until he gave a groan and held her away. 'Casey!' he admonished, but saw her laughing up at him and grinned back. 'You Jezebel! God, I'm crazy about you.' For a moment he continued to smile down at her, but then said firmly,

'Where's your coat? We're going to walk to the pub and have a drink.'

So they walked along together, Casey in a teasing mood that kept Reid laughing all the way, and for quite a while after they had reached the pub. It was only when he told her that he would be going away again the following week that Casey's eyes shadowed and she remembered the article.

'What is it?' Reid asked, taking her hand. 'Don't you want me to go?'

'No, I don't want you to go,' Casey agreed slowly. 'But mostly because of this.' And she took her hand away to take the article out of her bag and give it to him.

Reid's left eyebrow rose and he looked at her serious face for a moment before taking the piece of paper from her and reading it. 'Mm, very edifying,' he commented. 'I suppose Mark gave it to you?'

'Yes. Is that all you're going to say about it?' Casey demanded impatiently. 'Just "very edifying"?'

'What else do you want me to say?' Reid dropped the article on to the table and picked up his glass of beer.

'Reid, you could have been killed! As it is you've— you've lost the sight in one eye. You didn't tell me that it was that dangerous. You—you should have,' she finished on an accusing note.

'Why? Would it have made any difference?'

There was a challenging tone in his voice that made Casey stare at him. She thought about it and then slowly shook her head. 'No. No, I don't suppose so.' But she said it on an unhappy note and looked down at her hands in her lap.

Immediately Reid leaned across and took hold of her hands. 'Look at me, Casey,' he commanded. And when she did so, went on, 'Most sports have an element of risk, some more than others of course. And I'll admit that power-boat racing can be dangerous if you're not careful. But I *am* careful, darling. I've been racing since I was sixteen and this is the first time that I've been badly injured, and then it was purely bad luck. I hit the bow wave of another boat and it rolled me, that's all.'

Casey looked at him, at the constant reminder on his face of the crash. 'And what's to say you won't have more bad luck on your next race, or the one after that?'

'Nothing,' Reid admitted bluntly. 'But we're working to make the sport safer all the time. We're restricting the size of the engines to the weight of the boat so that they don't take off, and we're reducing the number of boats taking part in each heat so that there's less danger of them colliding. But most important of all, most drivers are having cells fitted into their boats. That's a kind of toughened shell that fits round the driver and protects him in case of an accident. It's saved a whole lot of injuries already.'

'And have you got these cells fitted to your boats?'

'Yes, of course. I don't want another crash. Look,' he said persuasively, 'my sister has invited us over to dinner on Saturday. Why don't we go over early and I'll show you round my factory so that you can see the boats for yourself? And I'll show you where I live, too. Where we'll both be living after we get married.' Adding, 'And I've found you a place nearby that I think will be suitable for you to use for your business.'

Casey was immediately diverted. 'We haven't got round to talking about that yet, have we? I'm glad you don't expect me to give it up.'

'Not at all. I don't expect you'll want to come abroad

with me all the time, so it will be good for you to have
something to occupy you. And anyway,' he grinned, 'it's
always good to have something to fall back on in case the
bottom ever falls out of the boat business.'

'Tell me about this place,' she commanded.

'It's in a converted warehouse that's been divided up
into units for light industrial use. There are several
people already there, and some of them are quite young,
so you would be in good company. I had a look over it,
and there's one unit which has very good natural light
which I think will be exactly right for you. But you'd
have to go and look at it and see what you think, of
course.'

'It sounds interesting,' Casey admitted, but there was a
trace of wistfulness in her voice. She had grown to love
her little cottage, and it would be a wrench to leave it.
For a moment she toyed with the idea of suggesting that
they make their home at the cottage, but Reid seemed so
certain that they would be living at his house that she
decided to wait and see it first.

When Saturday came round, Casey was waiting
eagerly for Reid to pick her up, feeling as nervous at
meeting his family as Reid had said he was at meeting
hers. 'Tell me about your sister,' she demanded as soon as
they were on their way.

Reid grinned. 'Her name is Elaine and she's married to
a doctor called Richard. They have two children; Emma
who's eight, and Paul who is six.' He gave her a glance,
then reached out to cover her hand with his for a
moment. 'Don't look so worried; they're going to love
you as much as I do. And I'm sure that you'll like them.'

Impulsively, Casey leant across and nibbled at his ear.
'I love you,' she murmured.

'Hey! Behave yourself when I'm driving, woman. Or I may stop this car and give you what you deserve.'

What woman on earth could resist a challenge like that? Her eyes dancing with mischief and anticipation, Casey began to undo the buttons of his shirt and slid her hand inside.

Reid pulled sharply into the kerb, switched off the engine, and turned to grab her. Pulling her into his arms, he kissed her fiercely, letting her feel his strength, dominating her, so that when he finally let her go she stared up at him breathlessly. 'Wow! Shades of Valentino. And just where did you learn to kiss like that, might I ask?'

He grinned. 'Behave yourself and one day I might tell you.'

'Oh, I see, a dark secret, huh! But I've an idea that you might tell me far more quickly if I *misbehave* myself.'

'Could be,' Reid admitted with a laugh as he re-started the engine.

They drove on and reached Waterleigh about half an hour later. Reid turned right at the crossroads and followed a signpost to Salford Lake, drawing up at the side of a very modern-looking factory complex which had three slipways going into the lake.

Casey got out of the car and looked round her in surprise. 'I expected to see lots of boats around, but there isn't one.'

'You're thinking of a boatyard where boats are repaired. Here we only build them.' Putting his arm round her waist, Reid unlocked a side door and led her inside.

It was a large, airy factory with boats of different models in various stages of completion. The hulls were

made of fibre-glass and Reid first showed her the large
moulds where the hulls were built up layer by layer, the
strong smell of the glue making her curl up her nose.
'These are the ordinary pleasure boats,' Reid told her,
indicating some smaller hulls. 'They're mostly used to
pull water-skiers. People put them on trailers and take
them down to the coast at the weekend. What we call the
weekender market.'

He led her on into another part of his factory. 'These
are the true racing boats,' he said with an entirely new
note in his voice. 'These beauties are anything up to forty
feet long, and I make them for two or three-man crews.
And those over there,' he pointed, 'are the cats.'

'Cats?' Casey asked in bewilderment.

Reid laughed. 'Sorry. Catamarans. Boats with twin
hulls.'

'And can you race these catamarans?'

'Most certainly. They're especially good for three-man
crews.'

Casey walked over to look at one of the sleek hulls that
was in the process of being painted. 'And this is what you
race?'

Reid shook his head. 'I used to when I did off-shore
racing, but now I concentrate on Formula One. And we
have different boats for that. Look, I'll show you.'

He led her out of the factory and across to another
building which was securely locked and fitted with a
burglar alarm which Reid had to de-activate. Taking
her inside, Reid switched on rows of fluorescent tubes to
light the windowless building, then took her over to a
boat that stood on trestles and looked as if it was in the
course of being repaired. For a moment Casey hardly
realised that it *was* a boat. It was so completely unlike her

conception of what a boat looked like, having more the appearance of a space shuttle than anything else. It crouched on the trestles, a machine built for nothing but speed, to propel the man inside it like a living projectile through the water.

'It's much smaller than the other boats,' Casey commented, lifting up a hand to touch the sleek sides.

'Yes, it's only about eighteen feet long.'

'And it doesn't feel like fibre-glass.'

'No, it's made of marine plywood.'

'How fast does it go?'

'It gets up to one hundred and fifty miles per hour.'

Casey had been standing with her back to Reid but now she turned to face him. Immediately Reid stepped forward and began to talk very fast to dispel the fear in her eyes. 'Look, this is the safety-cell I was telling you about. It's made of a composition called Kevlar; that's a mixture of immensely strong materials that protects the whole of your body. It's so strong that the American President has a bullet-proof vest made out of it! And the boat is fitted with a flotation system so that even if it goes under the surface it will come up again and keep the driver out of the water, so he can't drown. And then of course we wear life-jackets and crash helmets as well. It's really very safe, Casey, believe me.'

'So how come you got so badly hurt?' she asked disbelievingly.

'Because last year I didn't have the cell fitted to my boat. It's a very new thing, but already it's made a big reduction in the number of injuries.' Putting his hands on her shoulders, Reid turned her round to face him. 'Believe me, darling. Nothing's going to happen to me. It's no more dangerous now than any other sport. Not if you're good at it; if you know what you're doing. And power-boat racing is what I do know, nothing better.'

He kissed her on the nose and put his arm round her, and went on telling her how little danger there was until the troubled frown left her eyes and she caught some of his own enthusiasm.

'Do any women race?' she asked him.

'Of course. But not in Formula One. There are many different classes of racing, for different sizes of boats and engines. Often you get husband-and-wife teams, with the wife usually acting as navigator.' He grinned at her. 'Like to give it a try some time?'

'OK. But I don't guarantee not to be seasick if it's very choppy.'

'In that case I shall take you out on the lake where there aren't any waves,' Reid told her with a happy laugh. 'Seen enough? Let's go on to the house, then.'

They drove to Reid's house, although it was such a short distance away that they could have walked in less than ten minutes. It too was situated within sight of the lake, but it was surrounded on three sides by a rich screen of old trees that hid it from the road. It was a beautiful house; built in the reign of Queen Anne and completely symmetrical with a white-painted door and fanlight over it set exactly in the centre, and with two windows on either side, the upper storey having five windows to correspond. There was a stone balustrade at the roof level, partly hiding the slated roof, and it was set amid green lawns and beds thick with spring flowers.

'Oh, Reid!' Casey exclaimed in surprise and pleasure. 'It's—it's perfect.' She gazed at the house, unable to believe that it would be her home. She felt like a little girl who had been given a doll's house for Christmas, and was filled with an almost unbearable anticipation to open the front door to see what further wonders were inside.

Taking her hand, Reid ran with her up to the front door, unlocked it, but instead of leading her inside, stooped to pick her up in his arms. He grinned down at her. 'This is just in case I'm not in a fit state to carry you over the threshold when we get back from our honeymoon.'

'And why won't you be in a fit state?'

'Because I intend to be very, very exhausted.' He whirled her round, laughing as she squealed and clung to him. 'Close your eyes,' he commanded. 'Don't open them until I tell you.'

Casey looked at him lovingly, and kissed him, unable to resist it when she was so close, but Reid made a growling sound in his throat and she laughed and said, 'OK! OK! My eyes are closed. Look.'

'Good. Keep them shut now.' He carried her into inside and walked through the hall to a room at the back of the house before he set her on her feet and said, 'OK, you can open them now.'

She expected to be looking at the room, but Reid had stood her facing the french windows which gave a beautiful view out over the gardens down to the lake. The sun was shining, filling the room with light and warmth, making it feel almost a part of the garden and that wonderful walk down to the water, which glistened iridescently in the sunlight.

'This is my favourite spot in the house, the room where I have my breakfast every morning,' Reid told her. 'Either in this room or out on the terrace in the summer. To sit here, with that view, has always been a perfect way to start the day for me. Or I thought it was until I met you and realised that it wouldn't be really perfect until you were here with me, sharing it, giving it meaning.'

Misty tears gathered in her eyes as she turned to him. 'Oh, Reid, I'm so happy.' But then a sudden cold fear gripped her heart and she clung to him, trying to make his body part of her own. 'Promise me that you won't ever let anything happen to you. If it did . . . Oh God, I couldn't bear it.' Her hands dug into his shoulders. 'Promise me, Reid. You must. You must.'

'Nothing's going to happen. I swear it.' Reid's arms closed tightly around her, letting her feel the security of his strength and closeness. 'Nothing will ever separate us, my darling,' he soothed, his lips on her temple. 'We're going to be together for the rest of our lives. We're going to live here in this house, and we're going to raise our children here, grow old together here.' He lifted his head to look at her, the serious mood suddenly leaving him. 'That's so long as you guarantee not to prick your finger on one of those knitting-machines of yours and go to sleep for a hundred years, of course. Even I might get impatient waiting that long for you to wake up.'

Casey laughed at him, instantly diverted. 'But all you would have to do would be to find a handsome prince to kiss me to wake me up,' she pointed out.

'Won't I do?'

'Certainly not,' she said mockingly. 'You'd just turn back into a frog!'

That remark, of course, resulted in her being severely punished, if you could call being kissed by the man you love being punished, and it was some little time before Reid at last let her go and said thickly, 'Come and see the rest of the house.'

The inside of the house was as beautiful as the outside,

but it was too neat, too tidy. Only the room that Reid used as a study looked at all lived in. It needed a family to fill it. Looking at Reid, Casey realised that that was exactly what she wanted to give him.

'This will be our room,' he told her, leading her into a bedroom at the back of the house with a large lace-draped four-poster bed in it. 'It looks out over the lake at the back and over the shrubbery at the side. And it has its own bathroom through this door.' Reid glanced back at Casey, but she was standing looking at the bed. Going over to her he put his arm round her waist. 'Are you thinking what I'm thinking?'

She gave a small, happy smile. 'I rather believe I must be.'

'Good. I like a woman after my own heart.' He kissed her deeply, then took her hand and sat her down beside him on the bed. 'I think this is the right time and definitely the right place to give you this.' He took a small box from his pocket, opened it and took out a diamond engagement ring. Picking up her left hand, Reid slid the ring on to her finger and lightly kissed her lips, set into a round O of happy speechlessness.

From that moment the rest of the day seemed to pass in a kind of daze. They drove on to meet Reid's sister and brother-in-law and their two children at their modern house about ten miles away, and she liked them immediately. They made her very welcome, and brought out a bottle of champagne to toast their health as soon as they saw the ring on Casey's finger. Having champagne before they even started to eat made the meal itself rather a hilarious one, although afterwards Casey could only remember looking up often and finding Reid's eyes upon her, and the way he smiled at her then and reached to hold her hand lightly under the table.

It was, perhaps, the happiest day that Casey had known in her young life, and it showed. She glowed with a mixture of excitement and happiness that gave her a magical quality, a radiance that seemed to burn from within and make her prettiness become beauty. She laughed a lot, but her laughter often died in her throat as she looked at Reid and silently thanked all the Fates for the miracle that had made them fall in love.

Elaine and Richard watched them, then looked at each other and smiled, remembering their own courtship. Tactfully they took their children to put them to bed and left Casey and Reid alone together for a while. They went outside in the garden and Reid held her close to keep her warm, murmuring endearments between kisses, telling her how much he loved her, making the day end even more perfectly than it had begun.

The next day she rang her parents to tell them, and almost before she knew it the wedding was arranged as Reid had said it would be, for June, not even two months away. Life, then, became extremely hectic, without enough hours in the day to see to all the thousand and one things that needed to be arranged for a white wedding in such a short time. It was to be in Norfolk, of course, in Casey's local parish church. Reid had a talk with her parents and next thing she knew her mother had hired a large marquee that was to be set up in the garden of a local hotel, had booked caterers and what seemed like a fleet of white Rolls-Royces, not to speak of flowers, a cake, and invitations for a guest-list that seemed to stretch into hundreds.

'But Mum,' Casey wailed over the phone. 'It's going to cost a fortune! Dad will be in debt for the rest of his life. I

shall phone up the caterers and cancel if you don't
shorten that guest-list,' she said forcefully. And went on
arguing until her mother admitted that Reid had given
them *carte blanche* and told them that he would pay for
everything. 'Not that we'll let him,' her mother assured
her. 'Your father and I will pay what we can, but Reid
will pay for the rest. But don't you dare tell him you got it
out of me, Casey. He made me promise not to tell you.'

Casey replaced the receiver, fully intending to
telephone Reid immediately and tell him off, but then
she hesitated and slowly smiled, her eyes alight with
tenderness. It had been impossible for her not to find out
of course, but if Reid wanted to make their wedding day
as perfect as possible, then what right had she to deny
him? Besides, a great many of Reid's family and friends
were invited and they would probably expect a higher
standard than her parents could manage on their own,
she realised practically.

As Reid had promised, he had let Mark loose in one of
his boats, with the result that her brother was now so
enthusiastic that he spent every spare minute practising
either at Yarmouth or at Reid's marina whenever he
could get there. He talked eagerly of taking up power-
boat racing as soon as he left college in the summer and
had already taken part in a couple of races leading to the
local off-shore championship. When Reid heard this, he
made Mark almost as deliriously happy as Casey was by
promising him a job with his back-up team, which
travelled to all the Grand Prix races with him.

But Mark had to wait until he finished college and
Casey had to wait at home while Reid was away racing
for most of the weeks leading up to their wedding. He
phoned her every day from wherever he happened to be,

usually with the news that he had won or been well placed in his race. But, never having seen him take part in a race, it was an unreal world for Casey, and she was much more eager to discuss problems that had arisen over the wedding, or arrangements to take over the lease of the warehouse unit and move all her knitting-machines over there.

When he did come home it was usually only on a flying visit, and they were always so busy; meeting the friend who was to be his best man, shopping for wedding rings, ordering a new passport in her married name, going to visit some of Reid's relations who wanted to meet her before the wedding; they just never seemed to get any time to themselves. The only good thing about it, of course, was that it at least made it easier for them to resist making love until their longed-for wedding night. Sometimes it was terribly hard, when Reid came home and walked into the cottage, took her into his arms and kissed her with a mounting passion that filled them both with aching desire, setting their bodies on fire with the deep yearning that only sexual love could quench.

At last the day of their wedding arrived, and proved to be one of those beautifully hot days that give promise of the summer to come. Reid was staying at the hotel where the reception was to be held, with Elaine and Richard and the two children, who were to be page and bridesmaid. They were married at eleven-thirty in the morning with her mother unashamedly weeping and her father very close to tears himself. Casey wore an exquisite short-sleeved lace dress with a long, trailing skirt, and turned a radiantly happy face to Reid as he lifted the veil over her head. He wore morning dress, of course, that somehow seemed all wrong with that eye-patch, almost

as if her pirate had been tamed. She felt so full of love for
him, so choked by emotion that she could hardly repeat
her vows. Only when Reid's hand took hers could she
find the strength to speak coherently.

And then it was over and they were out in the sunshine
again, posing for the photographer and driving on to the
hotel to greet their guests and be photographed again
and again. Casey drank toasts to the bridesmaid and the
best man, to her parents and the little page. She shook
hands with innumerable friends of Reid, who often
turned out to be rival drivers, but close friends for all
that, who had come from many different countries to be
there. She introduced her relations and old school and
college friends to him, and he to her. The time flew by.
Mark came up, looking suddenly so adult in the morning
suit he had worn as an usher, apologising, but saying, 'I
must go. There's a heat of the championship at
Yarmouth today.' Casey laughingly scolded him and
kissed him goodbye, but then forgot him as they cut the
cake and she wished—oh God, how she wished—for long
life and happiness with Reid.

The cake was eaten, more toasts were drunk, and then
it was time to go upstairs to change, to throw her bouquet
into the crowd of her giggling friends, their hands
eagerly upstretched to catch it, and to escape to the car
through a storm of confetti, rose petals and rice that got
into their clothes and their hair, and even into their
shoes, so that they spent most of the time during their
drive to the airport trying to get rid of it.

But even when they got on their plane taking them to
California, Reid went to put something in his jacket
pocket and found that an enterprising guest had stuffed it

full of confetti that immediately seemed to scatter all over the plane, causing the people near them to smile in good-humoured sentimentality.

Casey sat back in her seat, her cheeks flushed with embarrassment, but much too happy really to care. She slipped her hand into Reid's, feeling the cold metal of the new ring on his finger. 'How long before we're there?'

'Hours yet. Too many hours.' His hand tightened on hers and he looked avidly into her face, both of them longing for the time when they would be alone at last, when Reid would slowly undress her and carry her to their marriage-bed, where all the pent-up passions of the last weeks would find fulfilment as he made her completely his wife. Their eyes promised a night of love and sensuousness, of yielding and possession, of giving their bodies to cement for ever the vows that they had taken that day.

The plane droned on through the long night and they slept a little, with Casey's head on Reid's shoulder. When they awoke it was day again and at last they were coming in to land. The wheels bounced gently on the runway and Casey relaxed, letting go her tight hold of Reid's hand.

They disembarked straight into the airport building and stood by the carousel to wait for their luggage before going to the Customs desk. The official there looked at their passports and then beckoned over a colleague who took their passports and said, 'Will you come with me please, sir? Madam?'

Mystified, they could only follow him into a small room where he turned and said, 'Mrs Lomax, I'm sorry, but we've received a message from England. I have to tell you that your brother, Mr Mark Everett, has been very badly hurt in an accident and it's feared that he may not live.'

CHAPTER FOUR

REID was magnificent. He cajoled the airline into turning off some of their own staff so that they could have seats on the next plane back to England, and arranged for a phone call to be put through to Casey's home while they were waiting. It was one of her aunts who answered, the poor woman so overwrought at having to talk to Casey that she was almost incoherent and only made things worse. Casey sat there, trying to understand, but her own mind was so numbed by shock that she could only repeat, 'What happened? How badly is he hurt?' until Reid took the phone from her and said firmly, 'Put your husband on the line.'

He listened for a while, asked a few questions, before saying, 'We'll be back in England . . .' he glanced at his watch, 'at six o'clock this evening your time. Arrange for someone to meet us, will you? Yes, to take us directly to the hospital. Goodbye.' Putting the receiver down, Reid took her hand and said quickly, 'Mark's alive. He's been taken to a hospital in Yarmouth and your parents are with him. He's had an operation and he's in intensive care. It seems that he's broken both his legs and he had some internal injuries; that's why they had to operate.'

He hesitated and Casey, her eyes fixed on his face, said, 'There's more, isn't there? Tell me.'

With a brief nod, Reid said, 'He also has head injuries. His skull is fractured and they're afraid there might be

76

some brain damage. That's what they're really worried about.'

She stared at him, her eyes very wide and dark in her set face. 'It happened in the race. He crashed, didn't he . . .' But she said it as a flat statement, not a question.

Reid's mouth tightened, but he nodded again. 'Yes, I'm afraid so.'

Casey went on gazing at him for a long moment, then she took her hand from his and clasped it with her other in her lap, looking down at the rings on her finger.

'Casey.' Reid went down on his knees in front of her, his hands on her shoulders. 'Sweetheart. Don't shut me out,' he said urgently. 'You've got to let me help you, comfort you.'

'Yes, of course.' She looked up and gave him a small smile, but her eyes were still dull with shock and fear, and Reid realised that she could think of nothing but Mark.

It seemed an age before they boarded another plane, their feelings so different now from the last time. The cabin crew had been told about them and came with offers of food and drink, of blankets and magazines. Casey shook her head dully, but Reid insisted that she have a brandy, and then took the blanket and wrapped it round her himself. 'Try and sleep,' he told her. 'Worrying about him isn't going to get us there any quicker. And you're going to need your strength when we get to England.'

Casey nodded, knowing that he was right, and she obediently shut her eyes and lay still, but she was far too anxious really to sleep. She could only doze fitfully, coming fully awake to the mental pictures of Mark crashing, of him lying in a hospital bed, his body torn and broken. She gave a whimpering sob and Reid immediately put his arm round her, holding her close against his chest as he gently stroked her hair, giving her the only comfort he could—that of his strength and closeness.

By the time they landed in England they had been travelling for over twenty-four hours and Casey felt deadly tired, although Reid, if *he* felt tired, hardly showed it. As they hadn't technically entered America, they didn't have to go through Customs, and their luggage was whisked through to where Casey's uncle was waiting with a car.

'Is there any more news?' Casey asked him anxiously. 'Is he going to be all right?'

But he could only shake his head. 'No, I'm afraid he's still on the danger list. Do you want to go home and change first or shall I drive you straight to the hospital?'

'Oh, to the hospital. And please hurry.'

Her uncle did his best, but no one could have driven fast enough for Casey in those circumstances. Her mind was filled not only with anxiety for Mark, but also with worry and sympathy for her parents, who must, she knew, be going through their own hellish torment.

When the car at last reached the hospital, Casey hardly waited for it to stop properly before she jumped out and was running towards the entrance. Reid shouted and came running after her and it was he who asked directions and took her arm to hurry her to the Emergency Ward. Her parents were sitting in the waiting-room, empty tea cups in front of them, both looking ten years older than when she had seen them last, when they had so happily waved her off on her honeymoon.

Casey flew to meet them as they jumped to their feet at sight of her. They hugged each other, tears running down their faces, her mother telling her what had happened in between apologising for bringing her home. 'We felt we had to let you know in case Mark . . . in case he . . .' Her voice broke into renewed sobbing.

'Oh, Mum! Please don't cry. He'll be all right, I just know he will. You know Mark; he's tough. He'll pull through, you'll see.' So now it was Casey's turn to give them what comfort she could, and it was quite some time before any of them remembered Reid, standing quietly by the door.

'Oh, Reid, I'm sorry.' Her mother got quickly to her feet. 'What must you think of us? And bringing you back from your honeymoon like this. Now it's all been spoilt for you.'

'Please.' Reid took her arm and led her back to her seat. 'My place is here with Casey, and to do what I can for you.' Sitting down beside her he said, 'Now why don't you tell us exactly what happened?'

It helped her parents to talk, especially her mother, and Reid was very good with her, encouraging her by telling her how Mark's helmet would have protected him, giving her the comfort that only a person with his experience of similar racing accidents could give, so that they soon began to look far more cheerful.

'Look, why don't I book a couple of rooms in a hotel?' Reid said persuasively. 'Then we can take it in turns to wait here while the others get some sleep. You don't want Mark to find you looking so tired and worried when he wakes up, now do you?'

Mrs Everett immediately said that she couldn't leave,

that she wouldn't be able to sleep, but Reid could be very persuasive when he wanted to be, and he had soon booked the rooms and cajoled Casey's exhausted parents into letting him take them there for a couple of hours' rest. 'Will you be all right?' he asked Casey in a low voice as he bent towards her.

'Yes. And thanks, Reid,' she said gratefully.

He nodded and kissed her lightly. 'I'll be back soon.'

When he had gone there was nothing to do but sit and wait. Wait to hear whether Mark had won or lost the greatest battle he would ever fight. But the doctors had told her parents that every hour gained would be to his advantage. But then would come the time when they would find out whether he had suffered any permanent brain damage, and they wouldn't know that until he recovered consciousness.

As Casey sat alone in the waiting-room, her heart torn by anxiety, it came to her that Reid must have been in a similar position to her brother after his accident last year. His sister must have been sitting waiting as she was doing now, wondering if he would wake to be a whole person or a living vegetable. Casey tried to imagine how she would feel if it was Reid lying there and not Mark, but her mind shrank from the thought in pure terror. And for all he had said that racing was much safer, it could quite easily happen to him again.

When Reid got back to the hospital half an hour later she was sitting quite still, her face very white, and for a moment he feared that Mark had died. Going quickly to her, he took her hands. 'Has—has there been any change?'

Slowly she lifted her head, horrifying him by the

bleakness in her eyes. But then she said, 'No,' and shook
her head.

Sitting down beside her, Reid took her hand and spoke
matter-of-factly. 'The doctor here gave your parents
some sleeping tablets, so they should be having a really
good sleep by now, and that will make them feel much
better. And I've had our luggage taken to the hotel, so
why don't you go back there and have a bath, try to get
some sleep?' He gently pushed her hair back from her
face. 'My poor darling, you've hardly slept at all. I
promise to ring you the moment there's any news.'

'No. You go. I'm all right.'

She continued stubbornly to refuse, so Reid stayed
with her until some eight hours later when her parents
came back, still anxious, but better able to cope now that
they were refreshed. Casey made a half-hearted attempt
to stay, but Reid took her firmly by the arm and led her
outside to the car. She blinked on the steps of the hospital
at the sun low on the horizon, her eyes sore from
tiredness. 'What time is it? I've lost track. Is it morning
or evening?'

'It's six o'clock in the morning. You're probably
suffering from a double dose of jet lag. The car's over
here.'

She went to follow him, but stumbled on the steps.
Reid turned swiftly and caught her, held her as she said,
'Oh God, I've never been so tired in my whole life.'

He supported her over to the car and again when they
got to the hotel and went up to their room in the lift. She
leaned against the wall as he unlocked the door and then
Reid simply picked her up and carried her inside,
shouldering the door shut behind him. It was a pleasant

room with a large double bed. Reid sat her down on it
and helped her to take off her jacket and shoes. He went
away for a moment and Casey fell backwards on to the
bed, but he came and sat her up again, and began to undo
her dress. 'Come on, darling, you'll feel much better if
you have a bath first,' he urged.

Dazedly she nodded and tried to undress herself, but
Reid's hands were far more deft than hers, taking off her
slip and tights with the ease that comes of experience.
Going over to her cases, he unlocked them and hunted
around until he found her bath robe. 'Here. Put this on.
I'll go and check on the bath.'

Numbly Casey did as she was told, finding it so much
easier to obey him than to think for herself.

'OK, it's ready.' Reid helped her into the bathroom,
then paused uncertainly. 'Can you manage?'

Casey nodded and he moved towards the door. In utter
weariness, Casey let the robe slip from her shoulders and
put her hands behind her to undo her bra, but it was new
and the clasp was stiff, her fumbling fingers couldn't
undo it and she gave a sob of frustration. Instantly Reid
was there again. 'Easy now.' He undid the bra and took it
off, hesitating only a second before reaching down to take
off her panties. 'Come on, in you get.'

He held her arm as she stepped into the bath and slid
down through the deep layer of bubbles into the
beautifully warm, soothing water. Casey gave a little
sound of contentment and leaned her head back, her eyes
closing as she relaxed fully for the first time in what
seemed days. 'Hey, don't go to sleep, Casey! Wake up.'

Reid looked at her lying in the bath, her breasts
encircled by the bubbles that clung wetly to her skin. His

jaw hardened, but then he rolled up his sleeves, knelt down beside the bath and, picking up the soap, began to wash her.

Casey forced open heavy-lidded eyes, murmured, 'Mmm, nice,' on a voluptuous note, and fell asleep again.

Looking down at her, Reid grinned ruefully. 'I'd hoped to be doing this to you in far different circumstances, my darling.' He kissed her nose and, unable to resist, bent to kiss her wet nipples, proud from the heat of the water. He went on washing her, enjoying her body, but driving himself half-crazy with frustrated desire as he did so, until he groaned and tossed the soap aside. 'Come on, Casey, stand up so I can dry you.'

She obeyed him protestingly. 'Reid, I'm so tired. Please let me go to sleep.'

'In just a minute, sweetheart.' Putting a large bathsheet round her, he began to rub her dry, his hands lingering longer than they should have done, his teeth gritted in frustration. Her uptilted breasts, especially, drew his hands and he just had to kiss them again. To his surprise, as he raised his head, Casey put her arms round his neck and kissed him fiercely. For a wild moment he was on the point of carrying her to the bed and making love to her, but the next second Casey's head drooped on to his shoulder and she fell asleep again.

It took a few harshly breathed minutes for Reid to regain control of himself, but when he had he quickly picked Casey up in the towel and carried her through to the bed and put her into it, not trusting himself even to find a nightdress and put it on her.

He stood looking down at her for a long moment, at the wet hair on her neck and the dark shadows of

tiredness and worry about her eyes. He swore softly but
vehemently at the Fates that had deprived them of their
wedding-night, that had ruined their longed-for honeymoon. Slowly he turned and went to have a bath himself,
then put on a robe and lay down on the bed beside her to
get what sleep he could.

When the phone rang a few hours later Reid woke
instantly and picked up the receiver before Casey was
disturbed by it. He spoke for a few moments, replaced the
receiver and turned to reach out to wake Casey. But just
as he was about to put his hand on her shoulder he
hesitated, seeing that she was in a deep sleep, changed his
mind and lay back again, his face troubled.

It was mid-afternoon when Casey finally awoke, some
noise outside dragging her back to consciousness. At first
she didn't know where she was, but then awareness came
flooding back and she sat up, full of anxiety. With some
bewilderment she saw that she was naked, and a glance
at the other pillow showed the indentation where Reid
had lain beside her. Colour burned Casey's cheeks as she
realised that Reid must have put her to bed, and hazy
recollections of her bath spread the blush all over. She
could hear Reid moving about in the bathroom so she
grabbed her robe and began to put it on.

Reid came into the bedroom a minute too soon and
caught a glimpse of her breasts before Casey hastily
covered herself. His mouth twisted a little in amusement,
but he came straight over to sit on the bed and kiss her.
'Hi. How are you feeling?'

'Much—much better.' Reid, too, was wearing only a
bathrobe and she was very conscious of this and of the
intimacy it created between them, that somehow seemed

all wrong. He put his arm round her and leaned forward to kiss her again, but she turned her head away and said abruptly, 'Is there any news?'

Reid's hand tightened on her shoulder. 'A little. Your father rang a few hours ago to say that Mark had come to for a couple of minutes, but not long enough for him to be at all coherent. But his unconsciousness now isn't as deep as it was, so they're hoping he'll come to again before long.'

Casey listened to him in growing astonishment and anger. 'Why didn't you tell me before?'

'You were fast asleep and I . . .'

'You should have woken me,' she interrupted forcefully. 'You promised to tell me the moment there was any news,' she accused him.

Reid shrugged. 'This was neither one thing nor the other, neither good news or bad. I judged it better to let you go on sleeping.'

'But you had no right to judge,' Casey exclaimed, swinging her legs out of bed and pulling the robe tightly around her.

Raising his eyebrow, Reid said shortly, 'No right, Casey?'

She coloured, realising that he was referring to the fact that they were married, but said, 'Not in this, no.' Going over to her suitcase, she pulled out some clothes. 'I'm going over to the hospital.'

'All right, we'll have a meal in the restaurant here and then go straight over.'

'I'm not hungry,' she told him, making for the bathroom.

Reid caught her arm. 'Casey, we haven't had anything

but a meal on the plane for over twenty-four hours.
We've got to eat.'

'You eat,' Casey snapped, pulling her arm free. 'I'm
going to the hospital to be with Mum and Dad.'

She put on her clothes in the bathroom, too quickly for
Reid, who was still dressing when she came out. Picking
up her handbag, she just said, 'I'll see you later—when
you've eaten,' and hurried out of the room.

'Casey, wait!' But she took no notice of him so that
Reid swore as he thrust his feet into his shoes and grabbed
his jacket and the things out of his pockets before going
after her.

He caught her up outside on the steps, where the
doorman was trying to get a taxi for her. 'It's OK,' he
said to the doorman and took Casey's arm to lead her
over to the car. 'Why did you run off like that?' he
demanded as soon as they were out of earshot.

'You said you wanted to eat.'

'Not without you. Surely you know that?'

'Why should I? After all, Mark isn't any concern of
yours, is he?'

Reid stopped and swung her round angrily to face
him. 'Don't take it out on me, Casey,' he said harshly.

Casey looked at him for a moment, stony-faced, then
pulled her arm away with an exclamation of impatience.
'Oh, for heaven's sake! Just let's get to the hospital.'

There was no change in Mark's condition. Her parents
were still sitting in the waiting-room. 'I think I shall
remember every inch of this place for the rest of my life,'
her mother said with a sigh as she took Casey's hand. 'Did
you manage to get some sleep?'

'Yes,' Casey admitted, immediately feeling guilty.

'Look why don't you go with Reid and have a meal while I take over?'

'That's a good idea,' her father agreed. 'We only had some sandwiches from the snack-bar here at lunch time; a proper meal will do us good.'

But Reid said firmly, 'Casey hasn't eaten, either, so why don't we all go? We can tell the people here where we're going so that they can contact us if there's any news.'

But neither Casey nor her mother would agree to this, so they ended up with yet more sandwiches and cups of coffee. Then there was nothing to do but sit and wait again, mostly in silence as there seemed to be nothing left to say. Casey sat next to her mother, holding her hand, while Reid sat opposite them, glancing through a magazine, but often looking across at her. Sometimes he caught her eyes and tried to hold them, but Casey refused to, looking quickly away.

Their stubbornness proved to be justified when, only half an hour after their return to the hospital, a nurse came in and told them that Mark had recovered consciousness, that they could go in and see him.

'Oh, dear God!' Mrs Everett immediately reached for her husband's hands.

Casey went to her other side, but the nurse said, 'Just his parents, please.'

Rebuffed, Casey could only stand at the door, watching them hurry down the corridor. Coming up behind her, Reid put his hands on her shoulders but she hardly felt it, she was so torn between hope and fear.

And it seemed as if her worst fears were confirmed when she saw her parents returning ten minutes later, her mother in tears and her father trying to comfort her.

'Oh no!' Casey breathed. 'Oh, please, God, no!'

Reid's arms went round her but she broke free of him and ran towards her parents. Her mother lifted her head and smiled through her tears. 'He's going to be all right, Casey. They say he'll get perfectly well again!'

Her mother was too overcome to go on, so it was her father who told them that Mark had recognised and spoken to them, that he had been lucid enough to do the simple tests that proved that his brain wasn't damaged at all. He had hardly finished speaking when the nurse came back and smiled at Casey. 'Would you like to see your brother now? Just for five minutes,' she cautioned.

'Oh, *yes*! Please.' She hurried after the nurse, hardly aware that Reid was following her.

Mark lay in the iron-framed bed, an oxygen mask over his mouth and his legs in plaster. His face was badly bruised and there was dried blood still in his hair. He was awake, and managed a feeble smile as she bent to kiss his forehead. Lifting the oxygen mask he mumbled, 'Hell of a mess, aren't I?'

'Oh, Mark!' Casey was too choked up to do more than hold his hand tightly, her eyes brimming with tears.

It was Reid who said bracingly, 'Don't worry, we'll soon have you out of here and practising for next year's championships.'

Mark grinned. 'You should have seen us go.' His eyelids fluttered tiredly and he let the mask fall over his mouth again.

Casey stood looking down at him, her face very white, then she turned abruptly on her heel to push past Reid and leave the room. But in the corridor she swung round

furiously to face him. 'How could you?' she demanded
with fierce anger. 'He's lying there half-dead and you
remind him about racing! You even encouraged him to
go back to it! It's nearly killed him once; do you really
think he's going to be fool enough to take it up again?'

'Why not?' Reid said evenly. 'I did.'

Casey glared at him. 'Yes,' she agreed bitterly. 'So you
did. But that doesn't give you the right to encourage my
brother to be as stupid as you.'

'Casey . . .' Reid began, reaching out to take her arm.

But she swung away from him, saying, 'Leave me
alone! Just leave me alone,' before turning to run back to
the waiting-room. 'I'm going for a walk,' she said to her
parents. 'I—I need some air.'

It was still sunny outside, the streets full of holidaymakers as Casey made her way towards the sea. The tide
was out, leaving a deep stretch of wet sand scattered with
seaweed and shells for the children to collect and play
with. She reached a flight of stone steps leading down
from the promenade to the beach and went down them,
taking off her shoes at the bottom to walk in bare feet.
Picking her way through the people, Casey skirted a
huge sand-castle and waited for the donkey rides to pass,
then walked on to the soft, wet sand, her feet leaving
imprints that immediately filled with water.

There was a pleasant breeze off the sea that lifted her
hair, and she put up a hand to run her fingers through it,
lifting her face to the sun as she did so. Once some
children splashed her, but she hardly noticed it, and once
two young men in the briefest of bathing trunks walked
along beside her and tried to pick her up, but the cold,

dispassionate look she gave them soon put them off and they left her alone.

Her mind was filled by the picture of Mark lying there; the reality of the broken legs, the oxygen mask, the metal frame on his head, and all the other apparatus that was keeping him alive, so different and so much harsher than anything she had imagined. OK, so he was lucky and he was going to be all right, but what luck had there been in having had the accident in the first place? It would be months before he was completely well again, and in the meantime what would happen about the exams he had been working for two years to take? And what about the work and hardship it would mean for her parents, who would have to do everything for him until he could walk again? He should never have taken part in the race, not when there was so much to lose. And maybe he wouldn't have done if Reid hadn't encouraged him, hadn't let him practise in his own boats.

Casey walked along until the beach thinned out and there were very few people, the noise of thousands of holidaymakers determined to enjoy themselves blown away by the breeze, until there was only the sound of the sea and the mewing of seagulls flying overhead, their underbellies pure white, their wings translucent in the sunlight. She turned and went to sit on the dry sand, looking up at the birds as they circled in the sky, riding on the thermals. She watched them for a long time, apparently absorbed in their activity, but her mind was on her brother and on Reid, her thoughts and emotions leading her to an unacknowledged decision.

From the promenade behind her, where Reid had been following her along, he stood and watched her for a while, then swung himself over the railing and dropped lightly on to the sand. Coming to sit down beside her, he said lightly, 'Hi. Remember me?'

Casey turned to look at him, somehow not at all surprised to see him. 'Yes, I remember,' she answered levelly.

'Good.' Deliberately he picked up her hand and carried it to his mouth, kissing her fingers one by one. 'Are you hungry yet?'

'Yes, I think I am,' she admitted, almost on a note of discovery. 'In fact, I think I could eat a horse.'

Reid grinned, a look of relief in his eyes. 'OK, why don't we meet up with your parents, and go out and have a bottle of champagne to celebrate Mark's recovery?'

Casey pursed her lips. 'I hardly think that's appropriate,' she said, getting to her feet.

Reid stood up beside her. 'Why not? He's young and strong, in a few months he'll have forgotten this ever happened.'

'And then he'll go back to power-boat racing?'

'Yes, if he wants to.'

'Just like you did?'

'Casey, I . . .'

'Reid, I don't want you to race any more. Please, say you won't. Please give it up.' Her eyes were on his face, wide and entreating, her voice so appealing that it caught at his heart.

But Reid stuffed his hands, tightly curled into fists, into his pockets, 'I've been waiting for you to come out with this,' he said shortly. 'You've been building up to say it to me ever since you heard about Mark.'

'And is it so unnatural?' Casey burst out. 'I love you. I

don't want to see you lying there like Mark. So ill. So hurt.'

'No, of course it's not unnatural. But you're speaking out of the emotions you're feeling now. You've been through a hell of a lot and you're punch-drunk and afraid. In a few days when you're feeling rested and when you see Mark continuing to improve, you'll realise that this isn't the disaster you think it is at the moment.'

'No,' Casey broke in angrily. 'I'm not going to let you talk me into believing that it isn't dangerous. Mark could have been killed and so could you. It could have left Mark as a vegetable if his brain had been damaged, and——' she hesitated but then added brutally, 'and it's left you half-blind. I'm sorry, Reid, I know you love racing, but I hope that you love me more. I couldn't . . .' Her voice broke. 'I couldn't bear it if anything happened to you. I just couldn't.'

'Nothing's going to happen to me,' Reid said firmly, taking a step towards her and catching her hands. 'Look, you've never even seen a race. Will you come to the next one, see for yourself?'

'No, I don't want to watch you. I'd be terrified the whole time. Just say you'll give it up, Reid. *Please.*'

His brow creasing into a frown, he said, tersely, 'I'm not going to discuss it now—you're too upset. Let's go back to the hotel and find your parents.'

'I shan't change my mind, Reid,' she told him defiantly, but he only took hold of her hand and walked her silently back along the beach.

Her parents readily accepted Reid's invitation to dinner in the restaurant at the hotel and each couple went up to their bedroom to change.

There was tension between Reid and Casey, although Reid did his best to dispel it by talking matter-of-factly about other things while they unpacked. Casey went into the bathroom to shower and put on a soft pink halter-necked dress, to do her face and hair and add matching high-heeled sandals. When she came out into the lamplit bedroom Reid, waiting for her in an immaculate dark suit, caught his breath, feeling again the familiar ache for her deep in his loins. 'You look very lovely,' he told her, taking her hand.

'Thank you.' Casey gave a small laugh. 'I'm also very hungry.'

'Let's go down, then. I expect your parents will be waiting.' But he couldn't resist drawing her to him to kiss her, and slipping a proudly possessive arm round her waist as they went down to dinner.

It was a quietly happy meal, all of them not a little tired with the relief that comes after a great worry has lifted. They ate their first decent meal in more than two days, and drank to Mark's speedy recovery in the champagne that Reid had promised.

'Although I feel guilty sitting here eating and drinking like this when Mark's lying in hospital,' Mrs Everett confided.

'Nonsense,' her husband chided her. 'He'd be the first to encourage you. Besides, he'll be able to eat tomorrow and you'll be able to take him lots of things in. All the things he likes.'

Casey's mother nodded, brightening, and looked across at her and Reid. 'And you two will be able to go on a belated honeymoon now that Mark's out of danger. I do hope you'll be able to get another flight.'

Casey smiled but didn't commit herself, and before long they all rose, and went up to their rooms.

'Who's going to have the bathroom first?' Reid asked lightly, taking off his jacket.'

'You can, if you like. You'll probably be quicker than me.'

While he was in there Casey took out the nightdress she had chosen for her wedding-night, beautiful cream lace and silk that contrived to be both modest and seductive. Taking off her shoes and dress, she sat down at the dressing-table and brushed her hair, then picked up her nightdress to go into the bathroom as Reid came out in his bathrobe. He held out his hand as she went to go past him and she stopped, turning to look at him. 'Don't be long,' he said huskily.

When she came out twenty minutes later, he was half lying on the bed. The curtains were drawn and only the bedside lamp lit the room. Getting quickly to his feet, Reid came towards her, his eyes smouldering with desire, his whole body taut with the strength of his need for her. 'Oh, Casey, you're so lovely.' Reaching out he gently stroked her bare arms, then moved his hands behind her to draw her towards him and kiss her with deep tenderness.

Casey stood very still, letting him do what he wanted, feeling his passion increase as he touched her, as he kissed her throat and her eyes, murmuring endearments, telling her how much he loved her. He put a hand in her hair and kissed her unresisting mouth with ever-deepening need. His hand was hot on her skin and she could feel the tension in his fingers, feel the tremors of anticipation that ran through his taut body.

She pulled a little away from him, her own voice unsteady as she said, 'Aren't you—going to put on your pyjamas?'

Reid smiled, his hand caressing her throat. 'I never wear them.'

'Oh.' She looked up into his face, having to tilt her head higher now that she wasn't wearing shoes. Her heart was thumping in her chest and her body filled with the ache of longing. But she loved him so much and love must come first. She had to tell him that. 'Reid,' she burst out. 'I love you. I love you more than anything in the world!'

'And I you, my darling,' he said raggedly.

He would have held her close again, but Casey put out her arms to hold him off. 'Will you promise me something? Please?'

'Of course. Anything.' His voice was thick and impassioned, little beads of desire on his lip.

'Then promise me that you'll give up racing. Please, Reid, if you love me, say you'll give it up.'

He grew still, his eye closing and his teeth gritted as if he was in pain. His fingers dug into the flesh of her arms as he said, '*Now*? Do you have to ask me that *now*?'

'Yes. I—I have to have your promise.'

Opening his eye Reid stared at her. 'And if I refuse— what then, Casey? What will you do?'

She gazed at him in consternation. 'But you said you would promise me anything.'

'But I want to know,' he insisted. 'I want to know what you would do if I refuse to give up racing.'

Casey blinked, then took a determined step away from him. 'Then I—then I should have to say that I won't—won't go to bed with you until you do,' she answered firmly, her chin tilted in defiance.

IT'S A WILD, WILD, WONDERFUL
FREE OFFER!

HERE'S WHAT YOU GET:

1. *Four New Harlequin Presents® Novels—FREE!* Everything comes up hearts and diamonds with four exciting romances — yours FREE from Harlequin Reader Service. Each of these brand-new novels brings you the passion and tenderness of today's greatest love stories.

2. *A Useful, Practical Digital Clock/Calendar—FREE!* As a free gift simply to thank you for accepting four free books we'll send you a stylish digital quartz clock/calendar — a handsome addition to any decor! The changeable, month-at-a-glance calendar pops out, and may be replaced with a favorite photograph.

3. *An Exciting Mystery Bonus—FREE!* You'll go wild over this surprise gift. It will win you compliments and score as a splendid addition to your home.

4. *Money-Saving Home Delivery!* Join Harlequin Reader Service and enjoy the convenience of previewing eight new books every month, delivered to your home. Each book is yours for $1.99—26 cents less per book than what you pay in stores. And there is no extra charge for postage and handling. Great savings and total convenience are the name of the game at Harlequin!

5. *Free Newsletter!* It makes you feel like a partner to the world's most popular authors...tells about their upcoming books...even gives you their recipes!

6. *More Mystery Gifts Throughout the Year!* No joke! Because home subscribers are our most valued readers, we'll be sending you additional free gifts from time to time—as a token of our appreciation!

GO WILD
WITH HARLEQUIN TODAY—
JUST COMPLETE, DETACH AND
MAIL YOUR FREE-OFFER CARD!

IT'S NO JOKE!

MAIL THE POSTPAID CARD AND
GET FREE GIFTS AND $9.00 WORTH OF
HARLEQUIN NOVELS — *FREE!*

CHAPTER FIVE

THERE was a shattering silence between them that seemed to go on for ever. Reid stared at her, his face suddenly drained of colour. 'My God,' he said at last, on a harsh, disbelieving note. 'You'd go that far?' She didn't answer and he said bitterly, 'And I thought you loved me.'

'I *do*. Oh, Reid, I do. So much. Can't you understand? It's because I love you that I want you to give it up.' She put a hand on his sleeve, almost shaking him in her urgency.

'Love!' Reid gave a harsh laugh. Suddenly he reached out and caught her arm, spun her round so that she could see herself in the full-length mirror attached to the wardrobe. 'Look at yourself,' he commanded, his hand tightening. 'Do you see how you look? But then you already know, don't you?' he added jeeringly. 'You know that you look seductive and beautiful with your hair brushed about your head and that nightdress clinging to you. And that lace . . .' His voice broke. 'You *know* how badly I want you. That I've been longing for this moment, when I'll make you truly my wife. Christ, Casey, I'd never have believed you could be so cruel,' he told her, dropping her arm, his voice full of pain and bitterness.

'I'm not. Oh please, Reid, try to understand. All the time we were at the hospital waiting, and when I saw

Mark lying there so badly hurt—all the time I was realising how I'd feel if it had been you who had been hurt. I—I couldn't bear it. I'm sorry if you think I'm a coward, but I love you so much that I just couldn't bear to see you hurt. And—and I couldn't live with that kind of worry.' She paused, biting her lip, realising from Reid's set face that her words were making no impression on him. Drawing herself up, she said more forcefully, 'I don't want to spend my life worrying about you every time you go away to race. Worrying about whether you're going to come home in one piece—or whether you're going to come home at all.'

Reid looked at her with cold but intense fury. 'You knew that I raced before you agreed to marry me.'

'But you told me that it was safe. And look what happened to Mark!'

'Because he's inexperienced. He's only a novice.'

Angrily Casey burst out, 'But you weren't a novice last year when you were hurt! What are you going to do— keep racing till you get killed? Or just till you're blinded in the other eye, too?'

His control snapping, Reid took a furious stride towards her. Casey backed away from him, but he caught her and dragged her to him, bending her backwards as he kissed her with savage anger. His lips pressed against hers until she had to open her mouth. His kiss redoubled its intensity, trying to force from her the submission that he so desperately wanted, his frustration driving him to a violence that he would never otherwise have shown. His hand went to the lace at her bodice, tearing it aside to reveal her breast. He strove to arouse her to a desire to match his own, tried to make her forget everything but the sexual need for fulfilment.

Casey gave a moaning cry and tried to push him away, but Reid bent her body back so that he could reach her breast with his mouth, one hand in her hair so that she couldn't struggle, the other pulling the soft silk away from her other breast so that he could fondle it while his mouth pulled and sucked at her burning nipple.

Desire flooded through her veins like an erupting volcano and Casey shuddered convulsively. Her hands went to his shoulders and she writhed under his hands and mouth, beads of perspiration on her skin, her mouth opening on a long moan of pleasure. Reid's fingers tightened in an involuntary movement of triumph as he thought that he had won, but from somewhere Casey found the strength to twist suddenly out from under him and break away. She began to run towards the bathroom, but tripped and fell on to the bed.

Reid came after her, grabbing her as she tried to roll off the other side and dragging her back. He put a leg across her, straddling her as he knelt over her, his robe hanging loose so that she could see his hard nakedness. Catching hold of her wrists, Reid held them on either side of her head, his face dark with anger and desire, his breathing ragged and panting.

There were tears in Casey's eyes and her voice was broken and uneven as she said fiercely, 'You can do what you want now, can't you? I can't stop you. But I—I won't be a part of it. You'll have to—to take me, Reid.' She glared up at him defiantly. 'If you want me, you'll have to rape me—unless you give me that promise.'

'You blackmailing little bitch!' For a moment his hands tightened on her wrists as his jaw thrust forward menacingly. 'I've a good mind to do just that.' But then his eye grew bleak and he suddenly rolled off her and stood with his back to her, desperately striving to regain control of his emotions, his knuckles showing white as he retied his robe.

With trembling fingers, Casey pulled the torn silk and lace across her breasts and sat up. She looked at Reid's back, hunched as if he was in pain, and waited for him to speak, not having looked further forward than this moment.

As if it was a physical effort, Reid straightened up and turned to look at her, his face so cold and withdrawn that Casey's heart felt chilled by it. 'All right,' he said acidly, 'you've stated your terms and I don't accept them. So what now?'

'You—you mean you won't give it up?'

'No.' It was a flat, categorical denial.

Casey stared at him in consternation. She had been so sure that he would capitulate. That his need for her would have been too strong for him to resist. On a desolate note she said, 'You can't—you can't love me, then.'

He didn't reply, just stood in cold silence and she felt her heart harden within her. But she lifted her head hopefully when he at last said gratingly, 'Yes, I love you. And I can understand you wanting me to give up racing. But I shall never forgive you for trying to force me into it like this. Not tonight. Especially not tonight,' he said bitterly.

Going over to the chest of drawers, he took a bottle of whisky that they had bought on the plane from the duty-free bag and poured himself out a stiff drink. 'Do you want one?'

She opened her mouth to refuse, but then changed her mind. 'Yes, please.'

Sitting down on the other edge of the bed, Reid handed her the glass, his eyes lingering on her broodingly. 'We could have sat down together and worked this out. It didn't have to be a head-on confrontation like this. However deeply you felt about it, Casey, it could have waited, because nothing is as important as tonight. Or it shouldn't have been.' Her hands had relaxed a little as she held the glass and the torn lace had slipped down, revealing the upturning curve of her breast. His jaw tightening, Reid went on, 'We could still discuss it in a couple of days' time. I could promise you that if it will make you happy. We could go into it, talk it through and . . .'

'No!' Casey burst out. 'You've already said you won't give it up, so what's the point?'

'The point is that we'll be lovers,' Reid answered harshly. 'In every sense of the word. There won't be any sexual tension between us. You won't be tired or anxious about Mark any more. We'll be able to talk things through rationally without—without these emotions coming into it. And without it being a form of blackmail.'

'You mean you'll just try and persuade and cajole me into letting you go on racing,' Casey said, her anger returning. 'I wouldn't put it past you even to use sex to make me agree to it.'

Reid's eyes narrowed. 'Isn't that what *you're* doing?' he pointed out coldly.

Casey turned away, biting her lips. 'It's different,' she said.

'Is it? Not in my book.' Reid reached out to put his hand under her chin and make her look at him. His face was still dark with anger that lay only just beneath the surface, the eye-patch giving him a cruel, barbaric look. 'If you love me, Casey,' he said deliberately, 'you will agree to forget this for a couple of days and let us make love now.'

She looked into his face, but could see nothing but the evidence of his past hurt. 'And if you love me,' she countered, 'you'll promise to give it up here and now.'

His thumb tightened for a moment, but then Reid took his hand away and took a swallow of his drink, outwardly quite calm and cold. 'So, we've reached an impasse. So now what do you intend to do?'

Casey looked at him unhappily, quite at a loss. 'I—I don't know,' she admitted.

Reid gave a harsh laugh. 'And nor, God help me, do I. It isn't a situation I've ever had to deal with before.' His eye went over her, saw the unhappiness in her face and smudges of tiredness around her eyes. 'Oh, go to sleep, child,' he said brusquely, getting to his feet. 'We'll talk again in the morning.'

Looking steadily up at him, Casey said, 'I'm not a child, Reid.'

His mouth twisting in bitter pain, he retorted angrily, 'My God, do you think I can't *see* that? Oh, hell!' He swung away from her and went to pour himself another drink before going to sit in the armchair. 'Go to sleep,' he repeated.

Slowly Casey put down her glass and turned off the

lamp, lay back on the pillow and pulled the covers over her. Reid was sitting in the shadows and she could hardly see him, but she was totally aware of him as he sat broodingly in the chair, occasionally lifting his glass to his mouth to drink. Turning her back towards him, Casey lay awake for a long time, wishing that she could cry. She longed to cry out her unhappiness, to have Reid take her in his arms and comfort her, but instinct told her that she had forfeited that right. That to turn to him for comfort now would only make him despise her more. Though why he should despise her, when all she wanted was his safety, she couldn't understand. It made her resentful and that helped, although somewhere at the back of her mind she knew that it had been wrong to do it like this. It wasn't too late; she could still say that she had been wrong, that they would do it his way. But Casey had far too much confidence in Reid's power of persuasion for that. She knew that if they got into a discussion about racing he would be able to talk so knowledgeably of safety innovations and percentages and practical experience that it was an argument she would never be able to win. That he would be able to shoot down all her protestations and end up twisting her round his little finger. No, this was her only way, her solitary weapon against his battery of charm and experience. But the bed was big and lonely without him and she so longed for his closeness and love.

Only when he was quite sure she was asleep did Reid come over to the bed and pull back the covers. Casey stirred and turned to lie on her back. The torn material had slipped from her soft breasts and the nightdress had wrinkled up as she slept, so that he could see almost the whole length of her long, slim legs. Pulling off his robe, Reid got into bed and turned off the lamp, lying on his stomach with his hands digging deeply into the pillow.

He was gone when Casey woke up the next morning. She dressed hastily and found him downstairs in the restaurant, having breakfast with her parents.

'Here she is, sleepyhead,' her mother said with a warm smile.

Oh God, she thinks I slept late because we were making love, Casey thought with a fierce blush. 'How's Mark? Have you phoned the hospital?' she asked to cover her embarrassment. She sat down in the only vacant chair, beside Reid, very aware that he had only given her one brief glance before turning back to butter some toast.

'Yes, and he's very much better. In fact they're moving him into a ward later this morning, so we'll be restricted to the normal visiting-times from now on.' She picked up the coffee-pot and began to pour some out for Casey. 'Now, what about you two? Are you going to see if you can get a flight back to America today?'

Casey put sugar and milk into her cup and hastily took cover in drinking it, not knowing what to say. But Reid gave her a wry glance and said, 'I doubt if we'll get a flight at such short notice. The airlines are pretty fully booked at this time of year. And anyway, I'm quite sure that Casey would much rather stay here so that she can visit Mark every day.'

Mrs Everett frowned. 'That is kind of you, dear, but what about your honeymoon? I really feel that you ought to ...'

'No,' Casey broke in. 'We—we can have a—a holiday

any time. What's important now is to cheer Mark up. We—it's all decided, Mum, really.'

'Well, if you're sure . . .' her mother said doubtfully.

'Of course,' Reid said with a smile. 'As Casey said, we can have a honeymoon any time. Can't we, darling?' he said deliberately, turning to look at her with a sardonic smile.

That false smile was almost Casey's undoing, but somehow she managed to nod in agreement.

'It's so very good of you. Both of you,' Mrs Everett said in deep gratitude. 'Mark will so much prefer your company to ours when he starts to get well. Oh, I forgot to tell you: the doctor said that they'll probably be able to move him to our local hospital in a couple of days. Then you'll be able to stay at home with us. That will be much better, won't it?'

Casey remembered the smallness of her bedroom and of her bed compared to the one in the hotel and gave a hollow smile. 'Yes, won't it?' she agreed.

That morning her father took Reid to collect his own car from the airport while the two women did some shopping and visited Mark in the afternoon, but they all went together in the evening. By that time Mark had fully realised the extent of his injuries and was feeling very depressed. They did their best to cheer him up, but he was feeling very sorry for himself, especially as he had lost all chance of taking any further part in off-shore racing for the rest of the season. Strangely, it was Reid to whom Mark turned, and he seemed to want to discuss his crash. It had been caused, he said, when another boat had hit a wave and had spun in front of him. He had had no chance to avoid it and he had been thrown out when the

two boats had collided. Luckily a rescue boat had been
standing by and had lifted him out of the water almost at
once.

'It's a pity your boat wasn't fitted with a safety cell,'
Reid remarked. 'Then you would have been strapped in
and you'd probably have got away with a few bruises.'
He said it deliberately and Casey knew that it was aimed
at her. Her mouth tightened, but she didn't make any
comment; this was neither the time nor the place to get
into an argument.

When visiting-time was over they walked to the
hospital car park where Reid and Casey said goodbye to
her parents, who had decided to drive to their home and
travel in to Yarmouth again the next evening. 'There is
such a lot of clearing up to do at home after the wedding,'
her mother apologised. 'And I want to get your room
ready for when you come to stay. Goodbye, both of you.
See you tomorrow.'

Casey was aware of the tension returning even as she
waved them out of sight. Reid stood silently beside her
and she slowly lowered her arm, her heart beating, afraid
of being the first to speak.

'Let's go,' Reid said curtly, and walked over to where
his own car was parked. He unlocked it, but then looked
over to her. 'You've never driven this car before; maybe
now is as good a time as any for you to try it.'

'All right.' Casey went round to the driver's side and
Reid showed her how to adjust the seat, his hand
accidentally brushing against hers as he did so. Casey
jumped as if she had been stung and hastily moved her
hand away, the physical contact more than she could
bear.

Lifting his head, Reid gave her a look of such sudden anger that her heart froze under its intensity. Her hands shaking, she gripped the wheel in fright and didn't dare to look at him as he went round and got in the car beside her. He closed the door, fastened his belt, and said shortly, 'Do up your safety-strap.' When she had done so, her fingers all thumbs, he said, 'Are you all right?'

'Ye-yes.' Somehow Casey got the word out, although she felt so nervous that she really didn't want to drive.

'OK, let's go, then. You might as well drive around for a while to give yourself a chance to get used to it.'

Forcing her mind to concentrate on the strange controls, Casey started the car and drove it very carefully out of the car park and through the town. The car was very different from her own old banger; it had a much more powerful engine and also had power-assisted steering which turned the car with only the very lightest of touches, whereas hers she had to pull round as if she was driving a tank. The windscreen wipers and indicators were on different sides of the steering-wheel too, which she found confusing, but after driving it for about twenty minutes Casey at last felt as if she had mastered it and relaxed a little.

'You're doing fine,' Reid encouraged. He glanced at her. 'Happy with it now?'

She nodded. 'It's just so much bigger and more powerful. How fast does it go?'

'In this country not faster than seventy. That's the speed limit, remember?'

Casey pulled a wry face. 'My old car would only get up to seventy if I had the throttle wide open, I was going downhill and I had the wind behind me.' Reid laughed and she said cajolingly, 'There's nothing about and this is a lovely straight road; couldn't I go just a *little* faster?'

He didn't answer for a moment, but then Reid sat back in his seat and said, 'OK, go ahead.'

'Really?' Casey gave a wide grin and put her foot down on the accelerator. The car picked up speed, but was still only cruising at seventy and was so luxuriously sprung that it didn't feel as if they were going fast at all. Casey gave a crow of laughter. 'Oh, you beauty. Can't she *go*?' She had regretfully to brake because they were coming to a road junction. She turned left to head back to Yarmouth along the coast road. 'Mm, that was *fun*,' she enthused, her face glowing with excitement. 'I've never driven that fast before.'

'Look, there's a track over there that leads down to the sea,' Reid pointed. 'Let's drive down it.'

Casey did so and stopped the car just above the beach. On their right the sea splashed gently against the sands and breakwaters and to their left the blood-red sun set the sky on fire as it died in beauty.

'So you like this car,' Reid remarked as she switched off the engine.

'Of course. It's a beauty.'

'And I think you'd have liked to drive even faster if you'd been able.'

'Why yes, I . . .' Casey broke off, realising where this was leading.

'Yes.' Reid nodded. 'I like to drive fast, too. But on water more than on land. And I get the feeling of excitement that you got then, whenever I race. Only with me it's magnified a hundred times because there's all the build-up to the race; the weeks of getting the boat in perfect running order, practising until you know the circuit, getting yourself into the frame of mind to win. Then there's the skill in trimming the boat exactly right, and other boats around you, the buoys coming up, and the thrill when you go round them first. Can you imagine how I must feel, Casey? Can you?' he demanded urgently.

Casey sat staring into the sunset, the colours so fierce they hurt her eyes. 'Yes,' she said huskily. 'I can imagine it.'

'And could you give it up, if it were you?' he persisted. 'Especially when you were about to achieve the peak of your ambitions?'

She turned to look at him, realising that she had been unwittingly drawn into the argument that she had always known she couldn't win. So instead of agreeing with him she said, 'Why did you marry me, Reid?'

His eyebrow rose. 'Because I fell in love with you, of course.'

'And did it never occur to you that what you were doing was entirely selfish? That you had no right to ask any girl to marry you when you were indulging yourself in a so-called sport that could maim or kill you at any moment?' she asked bitterly.

Reid drew back, his face hardening. 'Are you saying that you wish you hadn't married me?'

She looked away again, tears coming into her eyes, and mumbled, 'No,' as she shook her head.

'Casey, look at me.' When she wouldn't, Reid put his hands on her shoulders and made her face him. Seeing her wet eyes he gave an angry exclamation. 'For God's sake! Can't you see what you're doing to us? This ought to be the time when we're the closest, but your stubbornness is just pushing us apart.' Pulling her into his arms he said urgently, 'I want to love you, Casey. I want that more than anything else in the world. I want to be able to hold you close in my arms, to feel your body against mine. To touch you and say your name. To know that you're mine. Truly mine.' He spoke forcefully, his arms holding her, his lips against the skin of her throat as he sought to break her will.

'No! Leave me alone.' With a supreme effort Casey tore herself out of his arms, opened the door of the car and almost fell out on to the ground. Picking herself up she ran on to the beach, but she was wearing high-heeled shoes which soon slowed her down.

Behind her, Reid's door slammed. Effortlessly he caught her up and swung her round to face him.

'No,' she yelled at him again. 'Don't—don't touch me.'

But it was the wrong thing to say, only serving to increase his anger. With a snarl Reid dragged her into his arms. 'You're my wife,' he gritted furiously. 'I shall kiss you—and touch you—any time I damn well want to.'

He tried to kiss her but Casey twisted her head away. 'No. You're nothing but a liar.'

'What do you mean? What are you saying now?' Still holding her arms Reid pushed her away so that he could see her face.

Panting a little, Casey answered, 'Just now, you said that you wanted us to be—to be lovers more than anything else in the world. But it isn't true. If it were, you'd want it more than you want to race. But you won't give up racing so it can't be true.'

'Such typical feminine logic,' Reid commented with a

disparaging curl of his lips, then lifted his head to the skies as if asking the gods for help. 'Can't you see, Casey? It's nothing to do with that! It's a question of give and take. How would you have felt if I'd demanded that you give up your business?'

With a harsh laugh, Casey said jeeringly, 'I'm hardly likely to get killed using a knitting-machine.'

Reid gave an impatient exclamation and let her go. 'I suppose I was a fool to think that you'd understand. You're too young.' Shoving his hands in his pockets, he turned away.

'But not too young to know that I don't want you to get killed,' Casey told him angrily.

'That isn't what I meant. I meant that you're too young to see that using sex as a weapon is all wrong. You're driving a wedge between us, instead of bringing us together so that we can sort the problem out.' He looked at her tear-stained face and said tersely, his voice thick with emotion, 'Please, Casey. For the last time. Give this up. Let's go back to the hotel and go to bed together. Let's make love—and then work this out. I . . .' His voice broke. '*Casey, I want you so much.* Can't you *see* that?'

'Yes,' she admitted swallowing a great lump in her throat. 'And I want you. Desperately. But I have so much at stake. Your safety. Your life.' She made a small sobbing sound and her body shuddered. 'But everything's on your side. All I have is—is myself. Saying no to you is my only weapon.' With a sudden movement she ran to him and caught his arm. 'Reid, I don't want to hurt you. I want us to be together, to be happy. But I'm so afraid. If anything happened to you I wouldn't want to live. I couldn't—not without you.' A great sob tore through her and Casey put her hands up to cover her face, her shoulders shaking convulsively.

With a groan, Reid reached out and drew her into his arms, holding her close, his hand stroking her hair as he held her head against his shoulder. 'Don't cry, sweetheart. Please don't cry. It tears me apart.' He went on gently stroking her until her sobs had quietened a little, his lips against her hair.

'I'm—I'm sorry,' Casey mumbled. 'I don't—usually cry.' She lifted a finger to wipe her eyes, but Reid bent to kiss the tears away instead. 'I must look a mess,' she muttered as his lips traced the trail of a tear down her cheek.

'You look beautiful. You always look beautiful.' He licked a teardrop from the corner of her mouth and then kissed her with little exploring kisses that insinuated themselves into her heart and mind. She could taste the salt of her own tears on his lips and gave a last little sob that melted beneath the deepening intensity of his embrace.

Her arms went round his neck and Casey clung to him for comfort, for love. Reid kissed her fiercely now, and bore her back so that they were lying on the soft sand. He murmured her name against her mouth, his hot hands stroking her arms, cupping her breasts, moving on to follow the long length of her bare legs from her ankle to her thigh, his touch setting her senses on fire, making her gasp and quiver with awareness.

Her reaction increasing his own desire, Reid leaned pantingly over her. His body trembling as much as hers, he lifted his hand to undo the bows at the shoulders of Casey's dress, then dragged the material down to her waist. His eyes devoured her breasts and she expected him to fondle and kiss them, but Reid propped himself on one elbow and slowly undid the buttons of his own shirt, pulled it loose from his trousers and took it off. Casey's breathing quickened as she stared up at him, wondering what he was going to do.

Reaching down, Reid took her hand and lifted it to his bare chest. 'Touch me,' he said insistently. 'Touch me, Casey.'

Slowly she obeyed him, her hand gently exploring the smooth, hairless plains of his chest and shoulders, her fingers lingering on the hardness of his muscles, amazed that he should be so strong and herself so physically weak in comparison. She touched his throat, felt the pulse-beat that quickened even as she caressed him there, then moved on down his chest to circle the tiny nipples that to her amazement hardened with desire at her touch. She raised surprised eyes to Reid's face and he gave a small nod of confirmation. 'Look at yourself,' he murmured softly and lifted her head a little so that she could see.

Almost reluctantly Casey looked down at her own chest and saw that her nipples, also, had hardened. They were hot, too, and seemed to be alive with nerve-ends that cried out to be touched, to have their tenderness assuaged. She gave a little moan and looked up at Reid in unspoken need and helplessness. He laid her back on the sand, then lay across her, slowly lowering his body until their chests touched. Casey gave a gasp that became a tormented moan as he rubbed himself against her, setting her senses aflame, driving her to a fever pitch of desire. Suddenly his mouth was at her breast, making her cry

out, her hands tight on his head as she arched towards
him.

His hand went to her thigh, began to explore there and
Casey groaned, the exquisite torture making her writhe
and move voluptuously under him.

'Casey, say yes,' Reid panted against her ear. 'Darling,
say yes.' And he kissed her with fierce determination, as if
he would force the word out of her.

Her body on fire with the heat of desire, her breath
panting in her dry throat, Casey licked her lips, unable to
deny the crying demands of her own body any longer.
She opened her mouth to say the word he so desperately
longed to hear, but just then a shaft of light broke the
darkness and they heard the sound of another car coming
towards the beach.

Casey's mouth closed again and they lay still, hidden
from sight as they were in a hollow in the dunes. The
other car stopped for a moment, the driver probably
having seen their own car, then it moved off, parallel to
the beach, and drove on until it was out of earshot. But its
intrusion had broken the spell and brought reality
flooding back. Reid knew it as soon as he looked at
Casey's face. He swore violently and rolled off her, beat
at the ground for a moment in angry frustration, then
stood up abruptly and strode towards the sea. At the edge
he stopped and stripped off his clothes, then waded
quickly into the water, the iridescent caps of the moonlit
waves caressing his lithe, strong body.

As she watched him, Casey felt such a fierce pain of
longing deep inside her that she doubled up and had to
bite on her hand to stop herself from crying out. Oh God,
give me strength, she prayed. She wanted him so much.

To deny herself the pleasure of his lovemaking was as much a torture to her as it was to him. But it was his fault that they weren't back at the hotel making love right now, not hers, Casey remembered bitterly. Reid only had to say that he would give up racing and they could be happy for the rest of their lives, without the perpetual worry of his being injured or killed. Surely that wasn't too much to ask? And yet he was furiously angry with her for loving him, for wanting him to stay alive!

That thought left a bitter taste in her mouth, especially when Casey remembered how close she had come just now to yielding to him. She realised that she had absolutely no resistance to him when he deliberately set out to seduce her like that, her weak body an eager plaything in his hands, craving to be loved. So she must be sure not to get into that position again, she decided stubbornly. Until he capitulated she must be sure to keep him at a distance so that his hands and lips couldn't inflict their invidious devastation of her senses, couldn't make her forget everything but the need to make herself a part of him, to take his hard body deep into hers so that they would always be as one.

Reid came out of the sea and stood at the water's edge to dress, not bothering to turn away or even to see if she was watching him, drying himself on his shirt and then putting on the rest of his clothes before walking across to her. 'Ready to go?' he asked shortly.

Without answering, Casey got to her feet and walked ahead of him to the car, going round to the passenger side and sitting silently all the way back to town. When they reached the hotel Reid put on a casual jacket and they went up to their room, but once there, instead of getting

ready for bed, he put on another shirt and said abruptly,
'It's too early for bed. I'm going down to the bar for a
drink.' He waited for a moment, but when Casey didn't
speak, went out and left her alone.

Disconsolately, she took her time over her bath and lay
awake for a long time, but she had been asleep for over an
hour when Reid finally came back and crept into bed
beside her, careful not to disturb or touch her, and so
disturb his own hard-won control.

They both took refuge in being very polite to one
another the next day, being falsely cheerful when they
visited Mark in the afternoon and even more so when
they went again in the evening and her parents were also
there. Perhaps they were overbright, or perhaps it was
just the way that Casey was careful to sit on the opposite
side of the bed from Reid and keep well away from him,
that made her mother give them a sharp look. She
caught, too, the sardonic note that sometimes crept into
Reid's voice and the responding flush it brought to
Casey's cheeks, quickly hidden as she looked away or
began chatting to Mark again.

While they were there the Sister in charge of the ward
told them that Mark could be moved to his local hospital
the next day, and advised a day free from visitors to give
him a chance to get over the journey.

'That's marvellous,' her mother enthused. 'You'll leave
the hotel tomorrow, then?' she asked, turning to Casey.
'Your room is all ready for you at home.'

'You could come back tonight, if you like,' her father
suggested, finding the house empty with both of his
children gone.

'Yes, why don't you?' Mrs Everett joined in.

Casey opened her mouth to refuse, but Reid said quickly, 'That sounds like a good idea. We'll go back to the hotel and pack after visting-time and then drive over.'

Casey listened to him in some surprise; she hadn't expected him to be that eager to stay at her parents' home. Did he think that he might have more chance of getting her to agree to make love in the more intimate surroundings? she wondered. Her heart began to beat a little faster. How could she go on keeping him at a distance when there was no en-suite bathroom to undress in, and when her bed was only three feet wide and they would have to sleep in one another's arms if they were to sleep at all?

They went back to the hotel to pack, Casey folding away all her unworn honeymoon clothes for the second time. Her parents had gone on ahead and they followed about an hour later, arriving at the house just as the twilight faded into night. They hadn't spoken much on the journey; Reid concentrating on his driving and Casey, her pulses racing with an increasing kind of perverse excitement, realising that tonight would be the greatest test of her will-power—or *won't*-power, she thought with a hysterical inward laugh.

When they reached the house, Reid took her cases out of the car first and carried them to the porch. 'Is that everything?' he asked her.

'Of mine, yes, but yours are . . .' Her voice faded as she looked into his face and suddenly realised what was coming.

'I won't be staying here with you,' Reid said harshly.

'I'm going home for a couple of days and then I shall go on to America.'

Slowly, hardly trusting herself to speak, Casey said, 'To a race?'

'Yes. There's a Grand Prix race at Chattanooga on the twenty-first. I shall be taking part in it.'

'I see,' Casey answered shortly, trying desperately to keep pain out of her voice. Getting her key out of her bag she put it in the door and opened it. 'Then I suppose I'll see you when you get back—*if* you survive it,' she added cruelly.

Reid's face hardened into stone. 'Oh, don't worry, I'll be back. And when I do I shall expect you to have come to your senses and be ready to live with me as man and wife—in every sense of the word!' Then he turned sharply on his heel, strode back to the car and drove away.

CHAPTER SIX

CASEY stood in the porch for several minutes fighting off waves of giddiness, her breath harsh in her throat. She leaned against the wall, wanting to run after him and call him back, but knowing it was too late.

'Casey, is that you?' her mother called from the hall and came to open the door. 'Oh, there you are.' She looked past her. 'Where's Reid?'

'He—he decided to go back to his place,' Casey admitted, her mind too numb to be able to think up a lie. Bending down, she picked up her cases and carried them inside. 'I'll take the cases up to my room.'

'No, your father can do that. Is anything wrong between you and Reid?' Mrs Everett asked sharply.

'No, of course not,' Casey managed. 'As we can't visit Mark tomorrow, he decided to go and make sure the house and his business were all right, that's all.'

'You mean he'll be back tomorrow or the day after?' her mother demanded.

'Yes, if everything's OK,' Casey temporised, trying desperately to leave herself an excuse for him not returning.

'So if he's coming back why do you look like death? You're as white as a sheet.'

'Oh Mum, for heaven's sake!' Casey took refuge in being young and stroppy. 'I'm just tired, that's all. If Dad will take my cases up I'll go and unpack. Is there any chance of a cup of tea?'

'Yes, of course.'

Her father carried her cases up for her and went back to watch a television programme, but her mother came up later carrying a cup of tea and some biscuits on a tray. Casey's heart sank a little. 'You shouldn't have brought it up, Mum. I'd have come down to drink it.'

'It's no trouble. And you said you were tired, so I thought you might like to go straight to bed.' She crossed to the wardrobe where Casey had hung her dresses and shook her head with a sigh. 'Such a pity you never went on that wonderful honeymoon. I almost wish we'd never sent for you now.'

'I'd never have forgiven you if you hadn't. We can go again later in the year,' Casey said dismissively.

She sat on the bed to drink her tea, wishing that her mother would leave her alone, but Mrs Everett had opened the other side of the wardrobe, then turned to pull out the drawers in the chest. 'You've filled all the drawers!' she exclaimed. 'And the wardrobe. You've left no room for Reid to put his things in.' She stared at Casey for a moment. 'He's not coming back, is he? Is he?' she demanded, her voice rising.

Casey leaned tiredly back against the headboard. 'No,' she admitted flatly. 'He won't be coming back.'

'Why? What's happened between you?'

'Nothing.' Which was the truest word she had ever said. 'He's going on to America to take part in a race.'

'And I suppose he wanted you to go with him, but you wouldn't because you'd promised to stay and help look after Mark,' her mother declared, jumping to a safe conclusion. 'Oh, Casey, you should have gone! Your father and I are quite capable of taking care of your brother. And he'll have lots of visitors now he's so near home.' She gave an angry sigh. 'If only Mark hadn't crashed on your wedding day of all days.'

'If only he hadn't crashed at all,' Casey pointed out rather acidly.

'Yes, of course. But it was bound to happen some time, I suppose. Whatever sport he takes up, football, rugger or anything, he puts himself into it with so much enthusiasm that he was bound to get hurt somehow or other. I just hope he doesn't get hurt so badly again.'

Casey stared at her in horror. 'You're surely not going to let him go back to racing?'

The older woman laughed mirthlessly. 'You just try and stop him. He's got the bug now and nothing's going to stop him from getting into another boat the minute he's well enough. Just as nothing we could say would stop you from leaving home and setting up your own business. You're both extremely stubborn.' She stood up. 'Tomorrow I shall phone Reid and tell him to come back and get you. He can . . .'

'No!' Casey burst out. Then, at her mother's surprised face, she added more calmly, 'As you said, I'm very stubborn. I—I promised Mark I'd stay and I intend to keep it.'

'But you've been married less than a week,' her mother said in distress. 'How can you bear to be apart when you've only just . . .' She broke off, her face setting. 'Oh, but I forgot. You young people nowadays don't bother to wait for marriage any more, do you? I expect you and Reid were—well, more or less living together long before the wedding. So it doesn't mean so much being apart now.'

She went away soon afterwards and Casey got undressed and went to bed. How completely wrong her mother was, she thought wretchedly. She gave a bitter inward laugh, thinking that her mother would have been far more shocked to know that the marriage hadn't been consummated than she would to find that they had been openly living together first! In this day and age anyone would. Suddenly Casey wished fiercely that they *had* made love before the wedding, before she had fully realised just how dangerous power-boat racing could be. Then she would have had no weapon to hold over Reid's head. She could still have said that she wouldn't have sex with him of course, but instinct told her that it wouldn't have been anywhere near as effective. It would have been a cold, clean weapon rather than the instrument of torture she was using on him now. She tried to put herself in Reid's place and wondered what it must be like for a man to take his wife for the first time, but could only think how desperately she wanted that herself, and turned her head into the pillow to cry herself to sleep, the first time she had been able to do so since the wedding.

Reid phoned her the next day and again the following evening after they had got back from visiting Mark. But apart from asking how Mark had taken the journey and how they all were, there really wasn't much to say. But on both nights he said, 'Have you changed your mind?'

'Have you?' Casey countered.

'No. I shall be leaving for the States on Wednesday. If you need me—or if you change your mind—you can reach me on this number.'

He gave it to her and Casey carefully wrote it down, thinking that she needed him right here and now, desperately. But she merely said, 'Will you phone me when you get there?'

'Is there any point?' Reid answered, his voice suddenly becoming harsh.

Trying to control herself, Casey said shortly, 'I should like to know that you've arrived safely. And I should like to know whether or not you're still in one piece at the end of the day.'

'You know, Casey,' Reid said grimly, 'I'm beginning to think you'd like me to crash just to prove your point.'

'Oh, Reid!' Her voice breaking, Casey slammed down the phone, unable to talk to him any longer. Going into the garden, she cried until there were no tears left and then ran up to bed, merely calling out goodnight as she went up the stairs.

After that, Reid's calls were cold, courteous and brief. But at least he made them. He always asked her how she and her family were and she asked him how he was, but she never asked about the race. But on the twenty-first Casey never left the house, flying to the phone whenever it rang, her stomach a tight knot of anxiety. Her relief when Reid rang at the same time that night was enormous. For a moment she could hardly speak and Reid said, 'Are you all right?'

'Yes. Are—are you?'

'Yes, of course,' he answered, as if taking part in a Grand Prix race was commonplace.

His attitude after all her worry for him angered Casey. 'When will you be coming back?' she asked shortly.

Reid hesitated. 'There's another race in America in two weeks' time. Is there any point in my coming home before then?'

She had so been looking forward to his return that his answer infuriated her. 'Suit yourself,' she snapped back.

There was a long pause before Reid, his voice

hardening, said, 'All right, I will.' And put the phone down.

He didn't phone the next night, so on the following day Casey accepted an invitation to visit an old school friend and was out when he rang. His car had turned up on her doorstep the day he flew to America, driven up to Norfolk by one of his employees, so she was able to get around easily. Before, she had refused any invitations that meant she would be out when Reid called, but during the following week she accepted several, leaving her mother to answer when he rang. Her poor mother was completely torn: glad that Casey was enjoying herself, but worried that a bigger rift was growing between her daughter and Reid. 'You've got to talk to him yourself tonight, Casey,' she emphasised. 'He sounds—colder every time he rings. And Mark's college friends are breaking up next week so he won't need you quite so much.'

Which was quite a tactful way of putting it, Casey thought wryly. Actually she hadn't been needed at all. Whenever she had visited Mark there had nearly always been some of his college or boating friends there with whom he had far more in common than he had with her. Also, he had realised that she didn't approve of his racing, which put his back up. They had even come close to having a row about it, and Casey knew that her brother was no longer so pleased to see her when she went to the hospital every day. So living in the same house with him when he came home wasn't going to be any fun for either of them. And if she was honest with herself, Casey knew that seeing so much of Mark wasn't any good for her either, because it constantly reminded her of what might happen to Reid. Also it was getting to the time when they would have returned from their honeymoon, and Casey was beginning to be concerned about her business; she was bored with nothing to do and longed to get back to some physical work.

So she made a point of being home when Reid phoned the next day.

'What a surprise,' Reid commented icily when she answered. 'No invitation out to dinner with an old school chum tonight?'

His voice was heavy with sarcasm, destroying any heartache that Casey felt at the sound of his voice. 'No,' she answered tartly. 'You won't be able to reach me here again; I'm leaving tomorrow.'

'You're going home?' Reid said quickly, almost eagerly.

'Back to your house, do you mean? I don't have anywhere else to go, do I?' she said belligerently.

There was a tense pause before Reid said acidly, 'My house is your home, Casey. Our home—if you choose to make it into one.' She didn't speak, so he went on, 'You can pick up the key to the house from my cleaner, who lives in the village. Here's her address.' He gave it and said, 'I'll phone her and tell her to expect you tomorrow.'

'Yes, all right. I shall be glad to get back to my work.'

'Yes, of course,' Reid agreed sardonically. 'What else?'

So the next morning Casey packed her things yet again and drove down to Waterleigh with very mixed feelings. It should have been such a happy homecoming; the two of them returning from their honeymoon. She remembered the way Reid had carried her over the threshold the first time he had taken her there and the joke he had made about probably being too weak after their honeymoon. Wow! Did that joke sound sick now,

Casey thought bitterly, fighting back tears.

Mrs Grover, the woman who cleaned the house for Reid, was inclined to be chatty and curious, absolutely oozing sympathy when she heard that they hadn't been able to go away on holiday, after all. 'Such a shame,' she exclaimed. 'And how's your brother now, Mrs Lomax? I met him once you know, when he was down here driving one of your husband's boats.'

Casey got away from her as soon as she decently could and drove on to the house. It felt strange turning the key in the lock and walking into such a big, empty place, especially knowing that it was to be her home. She walked around, exploring, but feeling like an intruder, and it was some time before she went to the car to get her cases. All the clothes that she had left behind had already been put away in the wardrobes built into the dressing-room off the main bedroom, but when Casey went to unpack her case she hesitated. Surely Reid would take it as a sign of capitulation if she was prepared to share this room with him?

She stood looking at the big bed, remembering that this was where he had put the engagement ring on her finger, and tears filled her eyes again. She loved him so much and so wanted to have a normal relationship with him. Fighting him in this way was entirely against her nature; she was a warm and loving person and it broke her heart to have to be hard like this. But so much was at stake. If only Reid would give up racing they could be so happy. Casey gave a long, unhappy sigh, but then determinedly wiped her eyes and carried her case into a guest-bedroom at the front of the house.

The doorbell rang as she was busily transferring all her clothes from the main bedroom and she ran downstairs to answer it.

'Mrs Lomax?' A van from the local florists stood outside, its driver proffering a beautiful basket of arranged flowers.

'Yes, thank you.' Casey took them from him and quickly opened the envelope containing the card, fully expecting them to be from Reid, her heart beginning to thump as she thought that this might be a message saying that he had given in at last. It had been a wild hope and her spirits plummeted as Casey read the card. It said, 'Welcome to your new home. With love from Elaine, Richard, Emma and Paul.'

For a moment Casey was frozen with disappointment, and it was a while before she could think rationally again and wonder how Reid's sister had known that she would be coming to the house today. Presumably Reid had phoned to tell her. Which meant that he must at least be thinking about her. Her depression lifting a little, Casey took the flowers into the sitting-room and put them on a low table by the window.

The house was spotlessly clean and, once she had moved her clothes into the guest-room, there was very little to do, so Casey drove to the local shopping centre for a snack lunch and then on to the warehouse development where her knitting-machines had been installed. Reid had had her company's name painted on the board at the entrance, which gave her quite a thrill, and it was a wonderful feeling to unlock the door of her unit on the second floor and see all her machines set up and waiting for her.

The warehouse had once been used as part of a large flour mill and it overlooked a river that had been a busy commercial waterway serving the mill and several

large breweries further up the river. Her unit was very
light because it had a floor-length window where once
had been an opening where the sacks of flour had been
lowered to the barges waiting underneath. The iron
pulleys which had held the ropes were still attached to
the outside wall, but the river was now only used by an
occasional pleasure boat or canoeist. Its surface was
covered in green weed and its banks had gradually silted
up, making the river—which eventually flowed into
Salford Lake—much narrower year by year.

Casey spent her most contented afternoon since
Mark's accident unpacking her boxes of files and designs,
making sure the machines were working properly after
the move, and sorting out her boxes of wools and putting
them on to the rows of shelves that Reid had sent some of
his apprentice carpenters to put up for her. In short,
getting completely ready to start work again. She was
happy with the work-room; although it was not quite so
convenient as the room at the back of her old cottage, she
had to admit that it was far more practical, besides being
much larger. Several orders had arrived while she was
away and she was looking forward to starting on them.
She could work well here, she was sure of it. Casey's face
shadowed; she *could* if only she could stop worrying about
this situation with Reid the whole time.

At five-thirty she was about to pack up and go home
when there was a rap on the door and a man poked his
head in. 'Hello. Thought I heard someone moving
around in here. You must be Everett Knitwear. I'm
Johnson's Stained Glass,' the young man said, coming
into the room and holding out his hand.

Casey smiled and shook it. He was probably a couple
of years older than her, but it was difficult to tell because

of his dark, curly hair and equally dark, curly beard. He was wearing an old overall, liberally splattered with burn-holes, and his hand felt rough and calloused. And he had an eye protection mask pushed back on his forehead.

'I'm in the unit next door,' he told her. 'I've been here about three months now.'

'Oh, really? And you make—stained glass, I think you said?'

'Yes, that's right. Mostly windows for churches.'

'I shouldn't have thought there was much call for that nowadays.'

'Oh, you'd be surprised. There are quite a few churches being built; and the vandals who throw bricks at the old ones bring me quite a bit of business,' the young man said cheerfully. 'And what do you make on all these machines?' he enquired.

'Sweaters, mostly. Evening ones for the higher income bracket: I sell them to exclusive shops in London and the big towns.'

'Ah, for the rich bitches, you mean. You're very wise; that's where the money is, all right. All these pampered women with nothing to do all day but spend the money their husbands sweat their guts out to make,' he observed disparagingly.

'Aren't you generalising rather?' Casey asked with a smile.

'Probably,' he grinned back. 'What's your name? I can't go on calling you Everett Knitwear.'

'It's Casey. Casey Lomax,' she added, remembering. 'I—er—I got married recently.'

'Just my luck,' he remarked, raising his eyebrows expressively. 'All the prettiest girls get snapped up before

I get to them. You haven't got any sisters, have you?' he asked hopefully.

'Sorry, no. And what's your real name, Johnson's Stained Glass?'

He grinned. 'Well, it's really Justin, but I've been called Johnny Johnson ever since I can remember.'

Casey laughed and asked him how he got on with their landlords and they spent half an hour chatting and comparing notes about their respective art colleges.

'I started off my business in my father's garage,' Johnny told her. 'But he threw me out when I accidentally left my burner on when I was answering the phone, and set the garage on fire. Good thing, though, really, because it made me find this place. How about you?'

'I rented a cottage with a large room at the back, but this is much better.'

'How about your husband? Does he help?'

'Oh no, he—er—works up at Salford Lake. In a boat business.'

'He's lucky to be in work,' Johnny remarked. 'It helps to have a steady income coming in every week.'

'Yes, I suppose it does,' Casey agreed, feeling embarrassed by Reid's success and affluence, and not wanting to appear to be showing off by telling Johnny how it really was. She liked him and could see that they might become friends as well as neighbours. When they got to know one another better she could always let him know gradually. She glanced at her watch. 'I ought to be getting back.'

'Lord, yes! I suppose your husband will be expecting you home to cook his dinner. Lucky man.'

Casey laughed. 'You haven't tasted my cooking,' she joked.

Johnny closed up his own unit and walked down the central wooden staircase with her, revealing a pair of jeans and an old sweater beneath the overall. Luckily Casey had come in her own old banger and Johnny walked over to an equally ancient car.

'Do you live locally?' she asked him.

'Yes, just in the town. I've got a bedsit.' He pulled a face. 'It's not much of a place, though.' He looked at her hopefully. 'I suppose you wouldn't . . .' But then he broke off. 'No, you've got to get back to your husband. See you tomorrow?'

'Yes, I expect so.'

Casey drove home and made herself a solitary meal, almost wishing that she had encouraged and accepted Johnny's unspoken invitation. She could have done with some company of her own age. To laugh and talk, to get into arguments on every subject under the sun as she had in her college days. Sitting there, in the drawing-room of the big, empty house, Casey felt more alone than she had ever done in her life.

To break the mood, she phoned up Reid's sister to thank her for the flowers and received a general invitation to go over there whenever she felt like it. 'Don't wait for an invitation,' Elaine told her. 'You're family now. I shall expect you to come over whenever you feel that you can stand my brood.'

'Thank you, that's very kind of you,' Casey laughed. 'I'll be sure to do that.'

But as she put the receiver down Casey realised that she didn't feel like a member of Reid's family. Until she was actually part of Reid and he of her, how could she feel like part of his family?

She went to bed in the spare room but didn't sleep very well so she got up early, dressed and made some breakfast to take into the morning-room, the room that Reid had said was his favourite in the whole house. The early-morning sun was low in the sky, shining into the room. Casey opened the french doors and took her breakfast on to the terrace. It was going to be a beautifully hot day, even now the sun was warm enough for her to wear just a sleeveless shirt over her jeans. There was a light mist over the lake, which gradually faded away as it reached the bank and the long slope of rich green lawn, planted with oak trees, that led right up to the house.

It *was* beautiful. Casey sat there for a moment, just drinking in the sweet, fresh smell of the morning, feeling the sun warm on her bare arms. She put her hands behind her neck, lifting her hair, her head and body arched towards the sun like a pagan worshipper.

An exclamation of surprise sounded from the garden and Casey swung round, expecting to see the gardener or the cleaner. But it was Reid who was standing there, his mouth a little open, his arrested gaze fixed avidly on her.

'Reid!' Her glass of orange juice went flying as Casey pushed the table out of the way in her hurry to get to him. 'Reid!' She ran across the terrace and jumped down the steps into his arms. 'Oh Reid, I thought you weren't coming back. I thought you weren't coming back!'

She clung to him as Reid held her tightly in his arms, murmuring her name, saying, 'My darling, darling girl. Oh, Casey, sweetheart, I've missed you.' He kissed her hard on the mouth, moulding her body against his, as if the tighter he held her the more he could demonstrate his feelings. 'It's been hell to be parted from you. Especially when . . .'

But Casey didn't want to talk about that, not now, and she stood on tiptoe to kiss him back, kiss him with the avid passion that surprise had unleashed. There was no other thought in her mind than how happy she was to see him and how wonderful it felt to be held in his arms like this.

'Mmm.' Reid gave a long gratified sigh when Casey set his mouth free at last. 'That, I like.' He nibbled her ear and kissed her neck. 'You taste good. How about letting me eat you for breakfast?'

'Haven't you had any yet? Goodness, you must be starved. Sit here and I'll fix you some. Would you like bacon and eggs?'

'No thanks, just juice, toast and coffee.' Reid picked up her upturned glass and came into the kitchen to get a cloth to clean up the spilt orange juice. 'What did you do with yourself yesterday?' he asked her.

'I went over to the warehouse to get everything in order. Oh, and I talked to Elaine on the phone. She sent some beautiful flowers; they're in the sitting-room.' Putting the things on a tray, Casey carried it out to the terrace and they sat down at the table. However, by now the first exhilarating excitement at seeing Reid so unexpectedly had worn off and she was very much aware of the situation between them, growing more tense by the minute with apprehension as she remembered his threat when he left.

But Reid seemed content just to sit and look over the lake as he ate his breakfast, remarking on how well the garden looked and asking her about her favourite garden flowers and that kind of thing. Safe, uncontroversial subjects that made Casey slowly relax and revel in their first breakfast alone together in their own home.

'Tell you what,' Reid suggested as she stood up to clear the dishes away, 'why don't we pack a picnic and go out for the day? We could take a boat from the yard and go for a trip down the river.'

'In a power-boat?'

'No, I've got a small cruiser that I keep for Elaine and the kids to use. We could potter along in that.'

Casey smiled delightedly. 'I'd love that.'

'Great. I'll run up and change, then go over to the yard and bring it along to the mooring here while you get the picnic ready. Oh, and don't forget to bring a swimsuit,' he called out, already in the hall and taking the stairs two at a time.

The store cupboard and freezer were well stocked, so Casey just grabbed a basket and thrust bread rolls and fillings and fruit and wine into it. Then she ran upstairs to put on a pair of shorts, and hesitated only a moment before selecting the crocheted bikini that Reid had bought her a few months ago. She found some beach towels and, her arms loaded, carried everything down to the small wooden jetty at the bottom of the garden.

Reid was already in sight, at the tiller of a neat orange and white cruiser with a small cabin and a large cockpit, a boat built to take full advantage of pleasant summer days. He pulled expertly into the mooring and cut the engine, jumping off with a rope in his hands to tie the boat up while he helped her load everything aboard.

'Have you got glasses and a corkscrew and that kind of thing? I didn't know whether to bring them or not,' she asked.

'Yes, we're fully equipped.' He helped her aboard and they set off across the lake, Reid pulling Casey down on to the seat beside him, his arm round her waist as the breeze caught her hair and blew it around her head. He turned and laughed at her, apparently completely happy and at ease, and Casey's heart caught for a moment, wishing it were so. But if Reid could put their problems out of his mind then so could she, so she smiled back and moved closer to him, feeling the immediate tightening of his arm.

When they entered the river, Reid slowed right down so that their wash couldn't damage the banks, and now there was little or no breeze to lessen the power of the sun. 'It's going to be an absolutely perfect day,' Casey remarked contentedly as she looked up at the cloudless sky.

'I certainly hope so,' Reid agreed. Casey caught the innuendo at once, but he was already talking about something else when she gave him a quick glance. 'When the sun shines like this there's no country in the world as beautiful as England,' he was saying smoothly.

'I suppose you've seen quite a few?'

'Quite a few,' he nodded.

'Don't you get tired of travelling? Of being away so much?'

'I didn't before, because I had no one to come back to. Now that I've got you everything's different, of course.'

But, although she was nominally and legally his wife, he hadn't got her yet, not physically. So just how different was coming home for him? And what did he expect from this homecoming? But she had determined not to think about that and now, only a few minutes later, it was again on her mind. So to change her thoughts she said, 'Where are we going?'

'There's a small river that flows into this a couple of

miles further on. Where the two rivers meet there's a
small town, but then there's open countryside and it's like
going back about thirty years; no commercialisation, just
fields and meadows and one or two tiny villages until the
river gets too shallow to be navigable.' He smiled at her.
'There's a fridge in the cabin; how about a couple of cold
beers?'

They pottered on in the heightening sun, reaching the
town that Reid had mentioned. He pointed to where
another river joined the one they were on. 'You see that?
That's the river that goes past your warehouse
development.'

That reminded Casey of Johnny Johnson and she told
Reid about him, but presently broke off as they came to a
lock, an old Victorian one that lifted craft from one level
of the river to a higher one. Casey had never experienced
one before but obediently held the ropes that Reid put
into her hands while he worked the sluices that let the
water out. The boat sank slowly below the level of the
concrete lock and Casey's nostrils filled with the dank
smell of perpetual dampness and the thick green slime of
blanket weed that clung to the walls. But then Reid
jumped easily back on board and they were out in the
sunshine again and heading along a waterway between
lush green meadows and fields golden with corn.

They stopped for their picnic where a willow tree cast
dappled shade across a smooth, green bank, its feathery
fronds screening them from anyone who might go by on
land or water. Casey went into the cabin to change into
her bikini and they swam in the clear water for half an
hour, then dried off in the sun before moving into the
shade to have their picnic. They ate and drank
contentedly, talking a little but not much, each of them

careful not to disturb the peaceful atmosphere on this golden afternoon. After they had eaten they dozed, Casey's head against Reid's shoulder, but she woke when she felt his lips on her skin, tracing tiny kisses across her cheek.

Casey turned to him quite naturally, her arms going round his neck as she tilted her head so that he could kiss her mouth. He kissed her gently at first, savouring the sweet taste of her lips, the soft moistness of her mouth as his tongue explored it. Casey opened her mouth for him, then tentatively, deliciously, probed his in turn. His breathing quickening, Reid drew back his head, his eyes dark and intent. 'You look sensational in that bikini,' he murmured.

She smiled up at him. 'You chose well.'

'I could picture you in it the moment I saw it.'

But the next minute his hand was at the strings, undoing them and pulling off the top, for all that he had said he had wanted to see her *in* it. He fondled her hot skin, awakening an immediate response, but teased her for several minutes before he did what her thrusting body wanted and bent to kiss her breasts. Casey gave a long, shuddering sigh of satisfaction as she felt his lips close over her nipple, but soon it roused ever-increasing desire and wasn't enough. Her hips moved in voluptuous need as Reid lowered his hand to caress her there, her breath coming in little gasping moans. He moved to lie on top of her, only the thin material of their costumes between them, the hardness of his body a pleasure and a torment, too, as it pressed against her. Perspiration glowed on Casey's face and body and her breath became short gasps of moaning delight and discovery as Reid lifted himself on his elbows and pressed his entire weight against her, his body moving rhythmically. Every sensation, every nerve-end seemed to be concentrated in that one part of her. Growing waves of delight filled her senses, only to fade a little and then return with greater force until they suddenly engulfed her entirely in spasm after spasm of ecstasy. Casey cried out, her fingers clawing into Reid's back, her body jerking in a paroxysm of pleasure.

And then it was over. Casey gulped for breath as she lay trembling in Reid's arms, her body as wet as when she had been swimming. He stroked her gently until her thumping heart and ragged breath was nearer normal, giving her time to recover before he said softly, 'It can always be as good as that, sweetheart. Every time. When two people love each other as we do.'

Her hair still clung to her damp forehead as Casey moved her head to look at him. Hesitantly she said, 'Do you want me to . . .'

'No,' Reid put a finger over her lips. 'No. Not that way.' He gave a sudden grin. 'But I think I'd better go and have another swim right this minute.'

He plunged into the water and after a moment Casey found her bikini top and went in after him, but she felt weak, her strength drained away, and only splashed around in the shallows to cool off. Reid came to hug her in the water, but she splashed him until he retaliated and chased her, and they were easy and laughing together again.

They packed away their picnic and went aboard the boat to dry themselves, but Reid's eye-patch had got wet during their game so he took it off and put on dark glasses instead. He looked so different that for a moment Casey was shy, until Reid gave a mocking laugh and pulled her into his arms to kiss her. Then it was *definitely* the same man!

They took their time going home, stopping at a small village to go to the local pub for a drink and a meal, not arriving back at the mooring below the house until the sun was beginning to set after one of the most perfect days Casey had ever known. After they had cleaned the boat, they carried the things up to the house, and Casey would have tidied up, but Reid firmly took the things from her and put his hands on her shoulders. 'Let's go to bed,' he suggested softly.

Instantly tension came flooding back and Casey's heart began to thump. It had been such a wonderful day that for most of it she had managed to put the difficulties between them out of her mind. But now it was obvious what Reid wanted and that he had been trying to seduce her into a frame of mind in which she would yield to him all day long. 'Reid, I . . .'

But before she could go on Reid put his mouth against hers and picked her up in his strong arms to carry her swiftly up to the bedroom. But when they reached the landing she said, 'Please, Reid, I have to go to the bathroom,' and he reluctantly set her down.

Hastily Casey ran into the main bathroom and locked the door behind her, her fingers trembling. She turned on the shower and began to take off her clothes, intending to stay in there as long as she possibly could, but she had only been in the bathroom for a few minutes when Reid came and banged loudly on the door. 'W-what is it?' she quavered.

'Come on out of there! I want to talk to you.'

Even through the thickness of the door his voice sounded menacingly angry. Playing for time, Casey called back. 'I'm just going to take a shower. I won't be long.'

'You heard what I said, Casey. I want to talk to you—now.'

'What about?'

'Damn it, Casey, I'm not going to go on shouting through this damned door. Either come out here or I'll break it down!'

Hastily she grabbed up a bath-sheet and wrapped it round herself, but even as she did so Reid lost patience and put his shoulder to the door, making it strain against the lock.

'W-wait,' she called out. 'I'm coming.' And with her hands shaking with fright, Casey unbolted the door and stepped out on to the landing.

CHAPTER SEVEN

'WHAT is it? What's the matter?' Casey asked, trying not to let fear show in her voice.

Reid glared at her, his earlier gentleness completely gone. He was wearing only his jeans, his chest and feet bare. 'Just what the hell is the idea of moving all your things into the spare room?' he demanded fiercely.

'Oh, that.' Casey gripped the bath-towel tightly around her. 'I just thought it would—would be best.'

'Did you indeed? Best for whom? For you? So that you didn't have the bother of fighting me off every night, is that it?'

'No, it isn't like that. I . . .'

'No?' Reid's voice was scathing. 'So you did it for me then, did you? Out of the kindness of your heart, of course. So that I wouldn't have the added hell of seeing you with hardly any clothes on, of lying in bed beside you and not being able to touch you and love you. Knowing that you'll fight me off as if I'm some kind of monster when all I want is to be like any other man and love my wife!'

He paused for a moment, too angry to go on, and Casey said quickly, 'But you're not like other men, Reid. Other men don't go out and risk their lives just for—for passing glory like you do. Other men don't . . .'

Stepping quickly forward, Reid caught hold of her gesticulating arm and it was evident that he had hardly heard her. 'So I'm supposed to thank you, then, am I? Thank you for putting an even bigger barrier between us? A physical barrier this time. At least when we shared the same room and the same bed there was always a chance that you might come to your senses and see that what we feel for each other must come first. But now . . .' He stopped in disgust, too overcome by angry emotion to speak.

'I didn't mean it like that,' Casey said helplessly. 'I just wanted it to be easier for us.'

'Easier? I see,' Reid said jeeringly. 'And just how long do you intend to stay in there?'

'Well. Until—until you agree to give up racing, I suppose,' Casey admitted, her voice fading to a whisper.

'So it's just another form of blackmail, then. Your first ploy didn't work as you'd hoped, so you decided to put on the pressure. Put me through even more torment.'

'No!' Casey exclaimed wildly. 'I didn't mean it like that. I tell you, I did it for both of us. To make things easier. To—to . . .'

'Well, go on,' Reid said forcefully, taking hold of her other wrist. 'What were you going to say? To make it easier for yourself? Because it's just as hard for you, isn't it? You want sex as badly as I do. You loved what I did to you this afternoon, didn't you? Didn't you?' he repeated roughly, his voice rising.

'Yes! Oh God, yes,' Casey admitted with a groan.

'Then for God's sake why . . .' Reid bit off what he was going to say. 'No,' he said fiercely, 'I'm not going to beg and plead for what should rightfully be mine.'

'But I'm not too proud to beg,' Casey burst out and fell forward on to her knees. 'Please, please, Reid, give it up.

Don't kill yourself, *please*. You only have to promise and we can make love right now. We can go to bed and I'll do whatever you want, anything, if only you'll promise.'

'Why, you little bitch!' Reid pulled her roughly to her feet. 'What the hell are you trying to do—emasculate me before we even start on our married life?' His hands were trembling with anger, his breathing ragged as he glared at her, his eye-patch back in place now. 'Well, I'm not going to let you. And I'm not going to let you force me into taking you, either. But I've had enough of this, Casey. If you can't behave like an adult and sort this thing out rationally between us, then I'll just have to treat you like a spoilt, disobedient brat. And for a start I'm not going to stand for you sleeping in another room. We're going to sleep together as man and wife even if it is in the literal sense of the word and all we do is sleep. And you'll dress and undress in the bedroom, too, instead of sneaking off to the bathroom every time. What do you think I'm going to do, Casey? Go berserk at the sight of you in your underclothes? Or without any clothes on at all? Like this!' And he let go her wrist to grab the top of the towel and pull it off her, flinging it out of the way as his eyes went over her.

Casey gasped in horror and automatically tried to cover herself with her hand, but Reid grabbed it again quickly. 'Don't do that,' he ordered thickly. 'Don't ever cover yourself in front of me. After all, I am your husband,' he pointed out in bitter sarcasm. 'I do have some rights. And surely you wouldn't begrudge me the small sop of being able to look at you, even if you refuse everything else.'

'Let me go! Damn you, let me go!' Casey shouted,

struggling to break free of his hold, angry and humiliated.

'No, never!' Reid said savagely. 'I'm not going to let you shut yourself away in another room. You're my wife.' With a jerk Reid pulled her into his arms, then picked her up and carried her into the main bedroom. Pulling back the covers he dropped her none too gently on to the bed and held her down until she stopped struggling.

'That's better.' His free hand went to his belt and undid it, then to the zip of his trousers. He wasn't wearing anything underneath. Casey turned her eyes away and he laughed scornfully. 'What is it, Casey, are you embarrassed to look at me? Or is it that the sight of me makes you realise just what you're missing?'

Casey didn't answer and he got into bed beside her. He looked at her for a moment then put his hand in her hair and pulled her to him so that he could kiss her hard on the mouth. 'Goodnight, wife,' he said grimly. Again Casey didn't answer, and Reid laughed harshly and reached to turn off the light.

The blessed darkness at least cut his anger off from her sight, but she was acutely aware of the tense atmosphere it engendered around them. She was painfully aware, too, of their nakedness, and lay very still, afraid of arousing him again. She could hear Reid's harsh breathing, and almost feel the tautness in his body as he strove to control his emotions. How many nights had they lain together like this? Casey tried to think but couldn't. But it was too many. It would have been better if he had let her sleep alone, she was sure of that. But apparently that had been a slur against his masculinity, although Casey couldn't think why.

She lay stiff and still for a long time, her mind swinging from anger to despair. One of them would have to give in soon; they just couldn't go on like this indefinitely. Casey thought how it would be if she gave in now, this minute, if she reached out and touched him. That was all she would have to do, she knew. Just reach out and put her hand on him and Reid would turn and take her in his arms, give her the love that her body craved. She grew hot at the thought, her body trembling, her fingernails digging into the palms of her hands. But if she did that it would be a defeat. And how could she live with herself afterwards if she gave in so easily, so weakly succumbed to physical concupiscence? She had to be strong. If they were to have any kind of future then she just had to be strong now, much as she hated it.

But Reid was so stubborn. He said they could discuss it, but she had little doubt that he just meant that he would try to talk her round. He would make it all sound so reasonable, so safe; just as if taking part in a Grand Prix race was no more dangerous than having a Sunday afternoon round of golf. And once she had accepted his arguments and given in, he would carry on just as before. And somehow that would be an even worse defeat. It would mean that her love and worry for him were secondary to racing. That he wanted just a wife who would always fall in with his wishes, who would be willing to play second fiddle to him and have no mind of her own. And there was no way she was going to do that, Casey thought with gritted-teeth determination. She just had to win this battle for both their sakes.

She didn't know how long she lay so still, her body

tense, aware of every sound and movement that Reid made, but at last she fell asleep, only to have a dream in which she was walking naked down a busy street. She woke with a start, hot and flushed, and for a second was frightened to find that she actually was naked. But then she remembered and turned to look at Reid in the moonlight that filtered through the curtains. He wasn't there. The bedclothes were quite flat. To make sure, Casey tentatively stretched out her hand, but his side of the bed wasn't even warm. She thought that he might have gone to the bathroom, might be ill, but there was no light under the door. Getting out of bed, Casey went softly over to the door and looked out on to the landing, but that, too, was all in darkness. Perplexed, she stood for a few minutes, listening, but could hear no sound. For a ghastly moment she thought that he might have left her, have packed his things and gone, but then common sense reasserted itself; there was no way he could have packed without waking her, especially when she had been sleeping so nervously.

Casey bit her fingertip, wondering what to do. She would have felt better if she could have put something on; it felt so unnatural to walk about like this, but Reid might get angry again if he came back and found her with a nightdress on. The night was as hot and sticky as the day had been, so she walked over to the windows and pulled them open. They were full-length windows, giving on to a small, half-circular balcony. The faint lowering of temperature felt good. Knowing that the house wasn't overlooked, Casey stepped on to the balcony, its stone surface rough on her bare feet, and took a deep breath of cooler night air. There was a movement in the garden below and she drew back in alarm, but then saw that it was Reid.

He was standing about ten yards below the terrace, wearing only the bottom half of a pair of pyjamas, leaning one hand against the back of an ornamental garden seat. He didn't smoke and there was no glass in his hand. He was simply standing there looking up at the moon with a grim, hopeless kind of look on his face. As she watched, he lifted a hand to push his eye-patch aside and tiredly rub his bad eye. Love and pity filled Casey's heart and she wanted to cry out to him, to tell him to come and let her comfort him. But even as she opened her mouth Reid straightened up, squaring his shoulders, and she realised that he wasn't the kind of man who would accept pity from anyone, even his wife. So she stepped silently back into the bedroom and was lying in bed, apparently asleep, when he eventually came back.

They were both up early the next morning, the air between them brittle with tension as they ate breakfast.

'I'm going down to the boatyard today,' Reid informed her curtly. 'I expect I'll be there all day.'

'All right. I shall be down at the warehouse, of course.'

'Of course,' Reid agreed sardonically. He drained his coffee-cup, stood up and picked up his briefcase. 'See you tonight,' he said off-handedly as he left.

Casey didn't answer, just sat with both hands round her coffee-cup, staring after him and feeling completely wretched at the thought of another night like last night. She got up, suddenly wanting to be out of the house and away from this tense atmosphere. Quickly she locked up and ran to her car, not feeling at ease until she had reached the warehouse and was sitting at one of her machines. It felt good to be working again, to concentrate completely on what she was doing, and watch the sweater quickly grow under her expert hands. She worked solidly all morning, the windows wide open to let in the hot summer air, but at lunch time Johnny Johnson came and banged on her door, insisting she come and join him and most of the other people who had units there for a lunch-break. They all sat together on a stretch of grass at the front of the building, eating sandwiches bought from a nearby snack-bar, washed down with cans of beer and Coke. Johnny introduced her to everyone and she was soon deep in conversation with two girls who made kits for patchwork cushions.

Casey found that lunch-break wonderfully relaxing and pleasant after all the traumas with Reid, and she went back to work with renewed energy and enthusiasm, but when she reached her unit the phone was ringing. It was Reid. He said shortly, 'I've been trying to reach you for some time.'

'I—I'm sorry, I had a break for lunch. Did you—want me for something?'

Reid gave a short, derisive, laugh and she bit her lip as she realised what she had said. But Reid answered, 'I rang Elaine to tell her I was home, and she's invited us to dinner tonight. I said I'd phone you and let her know.'

'Oh, I see. Do you want to go?' Casey temporised.

Reid's reply was devastating. 'Anything would be better than just sitting at home acting like polite strangers to each other all night.'

It was a moment before Casey could speak, then, 'All right, tell Elaine we'll go,' she said shortly and put the receiver down, her hand shaking and all the torment flooding back, her temporary peace shattered.

She found it again for a short while when they went out that evening. Elaine and Richard welcomed them warmly, obviously quite unaware that there was anything wrong. The children were ready for bed, but had been allowed to stay up and see the uncle they adored and their new aunt, and for twenty minutes they all had a hilarious romp until Reid allowed the children to catch him and pull him down to the ground. Casey stood by, laughing, until the thought hit her of what a wonderful father Reid would make. Her face grew wistful and it was just at that moment that Reid stood up and looked at her, at once reading her thoughts. His mouth twisted and he gave her such a cold, cynical look that Casey hastily went down to the kitchen where Elaine was putting vegetables into tureens. She looked up with a smile. 'Has Richard put them to bed?' Then she saw Casey's face. 'Are you all right? Is anything the matter?'

'Oh—no. I'm—I'm fine, thank you.'

Elaine gave her a frowning look, but didn't press it. 'Dinner's ready. Will you tell the men?'

They ate in Elaine's comfortable candlelit dining-room, Casey and Reid sitting opposite each other. But all the tension was back now, somehow increased a hundredfold because there were other people there and they had to try to hide it. Reid succeeded quite well, talking apparently naturally, but when Richard asked him about his last race in America, Reid shot her a dark glance and said, 'I don't think we'd better talk about that; racing is a subject Casey has an aversion to.'

For a few seconds there was a startled silence while

Casey stared fixedly at her plate, but Elaine quickly broke it, like the good hostess she was, and said lightly, 'I don't blame her. When you men get started on power-boats you never know when to stop. Tell me, Casey, do you play tennis? We have quite a good tennis club near here that you might like to join.'

And so the tricky situation was glossed over, but they were all very much aware of it. After dinner they had coffee in the sitting-room and Casey quite deliberately went to sit in an armchair by herself. Reid gave her a sardonic look and went to sit on one of the sofas, a brandy balloon in his hand. Richard asked her how Mark was getting along and after she had told him he said, 'It was a pity about your honeymoon, but I expect you'll be going back to America with Reid when he takes part in his next race.'

Casey looked across at Reid, her chin coming up challengingly. 'Are you going to take part in another race?'

Without hesitation, Reid said, 'Yes. At Sacramento, next week. Don't you remember, darling?' he added with honeyed sweetness. 'I did tell you.'

'So you did,' Casey answered, accepting the challenge. 'And I think I remember telling you that I wouldn't be going with you.'

The air between them was so charged with volatile electricity that no one could miss it, and Elaine and Richard were far from being unobservant. They looked at each other quickly, then Elaine brought Casey's coffee across and perched on the arm of her chair to chat, while Richard went over and sat with Reid. After a while the two men got up and went into Richard's study to look at some business papers and Elaine put on a video film of their last holiday. It was mostly of the children enjoying themselves on the beach or in the hotel paddling pool and their antics soon had Casey laughing.

Elaine turned to her with a smile. 'You like children, don't you?'

'Why, yes, I suppose so. I haven't really thought about it,' Casey admitted.

'But you and Reid intend to have children? My two would love some cousins to play with.'

Casey's face shadowed. 'We haven't got round to discussing it.'

'No, I don't think we did, either. It's one of those things you just take for granted as part of marriage, isn't it?' Casey turned her head away and didn't answer. She very much needed some other woman to confide in and ask for advice, but to do so with Reid's own sister seemed wrong somehow. Elaine gave her a searching look, then changed the subject by saying lightly, 'How are you settling in to your new business premises? Several of my friends have admired my sweater and asked me where I got it, by the way.'

So the conversation was safe again and everything was OK until the men came back and Reid took Elaine's place on the arm of Casey's chair. Quite deliberately he put an arm along the back and rested his hand on her shoulder, his thumb idly stroking the side of her neck. Casey stood it for about a minute and then jerked her head away and sat forward on the edge of the chair where he couldn't reach her, like a frightened bird prepared for flight.

A sour look crossed Reid's face. Getting to his feet, he

said, 'It's time we were making a move. Thanks for your usual wonderful meal, Elaine, my love.'

They kissed each other goodbye and all walked out together to the car. Elaine walked round to Casey's side with her and said, 'Don't forget to come and see me any time you want some company or a chat, will you?'

Casey nodded and smiled, and it was only as they were drawing away that she realised there had been a meaningful tone in Elaine's voice. Did she suspect something? she wondered, and sighed; that wouldn't have been so difficult with all the tension in the atmosphere tonight. Especially after Reid had made that remark about her not wanting to discuss his racing. That rankled, and Casey burst out, 'Did you have to let Elaine and Richard know that we're having a disagreement about your racing?'

Reid gave a sardonic laugh. 'I would hardly call it a disagreement. Right now it seems to be an insurmountable barrier.'

'Call it what you like,' Casey snapped back. 'You still didn't have to let them know about it. It's private— between us.'

'Coming in between us, more like it.' Reid negotiated a turning into the main road. 'Look, do we have to go into this now? Can't it wait until . . .'

'No, it damn well can't,' she answered truculently. 'I want to know why you felt it necessary to . . .'

'All right, damn it!' Reid shouted at her. 'I don't *know* why I said it. Everything just got on top of me, I suppose. Sitting there as if we were a pair of happy newly-weds, when all the time we're growing more and more away from each other, turning what should be a warm and loving relationship into—I don't know, into enmity almost.'

'It isn't my fault. You've only got to . . .'

'Oh no, of course it couldn't possibly be your fault,' Reid sneered, his mouth twisted sardonically.

'Why you . . .' Without thinking, Casey lashed out at him in fury, catching him on the side of the head.

The car swerved and another car coming in the opposite direction hooted in alarm.

Reid straightened the car and braked to a violent stop. Reaching out, he caught hold of her arms and shook her, his face dark, his voice seething with fury. 'You could have killed us both!' he yelled. 'Don't ever do that again, do you hear me?' He glared at her, his breathing ragged. 'Or I won't be answerable for the consequences.'

He let her go suddenly, almost pushing her away from him as if he found her obnoxious. Then, after one last smouldering look, started the car again and drove on.

Casey fell back against her seat, frightened not only by Reid's anger, but by the strength of her own anger that had made her hit out at him. It shook her to think that she could feel such rage, that she could be so violent. She turned her head towards the window and put her hands up to cover her face, too appalled even to cry. She just wasn't like that, she wasn't a violent kind of person at all. But that was what this tension and frustration was turning her into, she realised miserably. And if it was doing that to her, then what was it doing to Reid? Whether it was true or not, from what she had read and heard, Casey had always believed that a man's libido was far more active than a woman's, and she could only believe that Reid wanted her far more than she wanted

him—and God, did she want him! It was like a chronic
ache deep inside her, always there, yearning to be
assuaged.

As soon as they reached the house Casey got out of the
car and ran inside, leaving Reid to put the car away. He
found her sitting in an armchair in the sitting-room, her
hands gripping the arms. For a moment they just stared
at each other until Casey said tightly, 'I'm not going to
sleep with you tonight, Reid. I just can't. I'm sorry if it
makes you mad, but I can't just lie there beside you all
night again!'

He took an angry step towards her then stopped,
seeing her drawn, set face and the dark circles under her
eyes. 'Oh, what the hell's the use?' He lifted a tired hand
to his forehead. 'All right, go in the spare room, then. At
least maybe that way we'll be able to get some sleep. I'm
going to bed. Goodnight, Casey.'

'Goodnight.' But it wasn't until almost an hour after
Reid had gone up that Casey finally dragged herself out
of the chair and went up to try to get what sleep she
could.

They were very polite to each other the next morning,
both of them finding that it was the only way to survive.
Luckily it was a working day and they were apart for
most of it and, although the next day was Saturday and
they normally wouldn't have worked, they each found
that they had a great deal to do and went into work that
day, too. On Saturday night they went to the theatre and
managed to escape for a few blessed hours into the latest
comedy hit, but as soon as they were alone again the
friction returned, accentuated by the comparison.

They went upstairs and Casey went to walk into the

spare room, but Reid put out a hand to stop her. Immediately she flinched away as if she couldn't bear his touch.

His face the grimmest she had ever seen it, Reid snarled, 'It's all right, I'm not going to force myself on you. You should know that by now. I merely wanted to tell you that I shall be leaving for America early tomorrow morning. If you want to use my car while I'm away, you'll have to drive me to the airport, otherwise I'll leave it in the car park there.'

'No, thank you,' Casey answered stiltedly. 'I can manage with my own car. What time is your flight?'

He gave a mirthless laugh that was heavy with self-irony. 'I haven't booked it yet. I just think it will be better for both of us if I go now instead of next week.' He looked at her, his face suddenly suffused with sadness. 'And God help me, but I don't think I can trust myself if I stay here any longer.'

When Casey awoke the next morning he was gone. The sound of his car woke her and she ran first to the window and then to his room. He had left it very neat, the bed made. When she pulled back the covers they were still warm. In a sudden orgy of despair Casey tore off her nightdress and fell into the bed, pressing her naked body fiercely against the sheets, trying to make his warmth a part of her if she could make nothing else, tears of unhappiness pouring down her face.

She went to work the following week mainly because she didn't want to be alone; even her motivation to work was dying now beneath her unhappiness, and she would sit idly at her machine or drawing-board, gazing unseeingly at the wall. But a couple of days later she had an unexpected visitor. There was a brief knock at her door and Elaine came in. 'Hello. I do hope you don't mind me dropping in. I've been dying to see where you work.'

'Of course not.' Casey recovered from her surprise and gave her sister-in-law a warm smile of welcome.

'Are you terribly busy?'

Looking down at the garment she was making, Casey realised that she had done hardly anything to it in the last hour. She shook her head. 'Would you like me to show you round?'

She did so diffidently at first, thinking that Elaine was just being polite, but she showed such a lively, intelligent interest that the two were soon talking in absorbed rapport, Elaine coming up with some marketing ideas that were really original. 'Perhaps I could help you a little on the sales side?' she suggested. 'Of course, it couldn't be until September; I'm tied to the house until the kids go back to school, but I'd really love to have an outside interest like this. That's if you don't mind, of course?'

'No, of course not. I'll be glad of some help. We'll work something out.'

'Have you got many orders?'

'Yes, quite a few. They're beginning to pile up a bit. I—I haven't felt terribly much like working lately. It's the summer, I suppose.'

Elaine gave her a quick look. 'Are you worrying about Reid?'

Casey's hands tightened on the ball of wool she was holding. 'Of course not. I'm sure he's quite capable of taking care of himself.'

'That's what all men say. But it doesn't stop us wives from worrying. I had a real go at Reid after his accident last year. I wanted him to retire from racing, but he assured me that it's much safer now.'

'Assurance is easy,' Casey said stiltedly. 'And very convenient—for Reid.'

'Oh, I didn't just take his word for it. I made him show me his new boat with the built-in safety-cell. I even made him take me to the place where they fit them and saw a couple of boats being deliberately crashed, but the drivers came up safe every time.'

So this was what Elaine had really come for, Casey thought angrily, to add her voice and persuasions to Reid's cause. 'I'm sure Reid will be pleased that you've come here on his behalf,' she began angrily, 'but I prefer to make up my own mind, thanks all the same.'

'I didn't,' Elaine put in swiftly. 'But I admit that I could see you were both far from happy, and it wasn't difficult to guess that Reid's addiction to racing is the cause. Good heavens, it's common enough. I know of half a dozen women who have left their husbands because they just can't take the stress of it any longer.'

Casey turned and stared at the older girl. 'You do?'

'Yes, and I don't blame you, Casey. But Reid has only had that one serious accident in about sixteen years. Because he's good, really good. And he wants to win the championship this year, very much. For himself, for his country—and for you.'

'For me? Oh, no, I . . .'

'Yes, for you,' Elaine insisted. 'Because he loves you so much. No one has ever won the championship three

times before, you see. I think he'd be very proud to give
you that.'

'I don't want any damn championship!' Casey burst
out. 'I just want him to be like any other man, and come
home safely every night!'

'Then you shouldn't have married him,' Elaine said
shortly, making Casey stare at her in astonishment. 'You
knew that Reid raced before you married him, and he's
not going to change. He loves racing too much. He's not
going to quit before he's ready. Especially when he's
worked so hard to bring in all the new safety rules. If he
gave up now it would seem that he had no faith in the
safety measures. That he was afraid, even. And that
wouldn't be fair to him because he's the most fearless man
I know.'

'I don't *want* a fearless man,' Casey said fiercely. 'I
want a *live* one.'

Elaine's face hardened. 'Casey, you've got to come to
terms with the fact that Reid's a man—the kind of man
who has the nerve to risk his neck for a sport he loves.
Would you really want him any other way? Would you
really feel the same way about him if he submissively
gave in to you and took up bowls or something instead?'
She paused, but Casey wouldn't look at her. 'Do you
think it didn't take courage for Reid to go back to racing
after his accident? It did, but he's very sensible too; he
made darned sure that he took every precaution he
possibly could against it happening again.'

Casey shook her head. 'There's really no point in going
on, Elaine. I realise that you're on his side and that
you . . .'

'Oh, rubbish!' Elaine stamped her elegantly shod foot,

'I'm not on anyone's side. But it's plain to see that you're both in a highly emotional state. You both looked drawn and unhappy when you came over to see us. Look, I don't know what kind of threat you're holding over Reid, but you've only got to look in the mirror to see what it's doing to you. And don't you realise what you're doing to Reid? You're getting him into such an emotional state that he won't be able to concentrate and will have an accident anyway. Is that what you want, Casey?'

'No, of course not,' Casey said vehemently. 'But when my brother had that crash I could see that it could easily have happened to Reid. And if anything happened to him I couldn't bear it.'

Elaine nodded sadly. 'I can understand that. But you're not going to change him, Casey. Especially not this way. You've got to be as brave as he is. And if you go on with this—well, then I think you're going to have to be very careful you don't lose him altogether.'

She left then, leaving Casey staring after her with a stunned look on her face. She hadn't allowed herself to think that Reid wouldn't capitulate or what would happen if he didn't. She sat down, trying for the first time really to look into the future, only slowly realising that there just wasn't any future in the way they were heading. They would just put up more and more barriers, build thicker walls of icy politeness until they froze out the love they had had for each other and found that they were happier apart. Casey's own heart grew cold at the prospect and she reluctantly began to ponder over what Elaine had said.

Reid still rang her every night, although they had less and less to say to each other, but when he rang that evening, Casey said abruptly, 'Elaine came to see me at the warehouse today. Did you send her?'

Reid's voice was immediately wary. 'No. Why, what did she say?'

'An awful lot about you. About racing. About how she wanted you to give it up and you wouldn't. It seems that you don't listen to anyone who loves you.'

'Do you love me, Casey?'

Her voice broke. 'You know I do. But when I ask you—beg you to give up racing you just get angry with me. You're angry with me for loving you, for wanting you to live.'

Reid was silent for such a long moment that for a few breathless seconds Casey thought that she had won, that he was going to give in. But he sighed tiredly and said, 'Did Elaine say that she was still unhappy at my racing, that she still wants me to give it up?'

It was Casey's turn to be silent, wishing she could lie, but, 'No,' she admitted abruptly. 'She said you'd convinced her that it was safer.'

'No, not convinced, Casey,' Reid put in quickly, '*proved* to her. I did for her what I've all along wanted to do for you; take you and show you a boat being crashed and how the new safety-cell and flotation system protects the driver. Will you let me do that, Casey? Will you? Please?'

Casey sighed wearily. 'Oh, I don't know. I just don't know. After your accident and Mark's, I don't see how I can ever have any peace of mind.'

'You will, sweetheart, I promise you,' Reid declared, a new note of hope in his voice. 'Look, don't worry about it now. I'll be home soon and we'll talk about it then.'

'When will you be home?'

'In a couple of days. I've just got to see that my boat is safely put on the plane back to England.'

'The race is over?'

'Yes.'

Casey hesitated and then, even though she only dimly realised it, took a tremendous step towards solving their problems. 'Did you win?'

There was an undercurrent of happiness behind Reid's ruefulness as he said, 'No. I only came fourth. I mustn't have been concentrating or something.'

'You weren't—you weren't hurt?'

His voice was warm, reassuring. 'No, no one was hurt at all. One boat went over, but the driver was OK.'

'I see.' She hesitated and it was almost a physical effort to speak the words that she felt to be a betrayal of the love she held for him. 'All right, Reid. When—when you get home we'll—talk about it.' And she put the phone down before she could possibly hear the jubilation in his voice.

CHAPTER EIGHT

IT was with a much lighter step that Reid walked into the house in the early evening two days later. Casey was in the kitchen preparing a meal, and he came straight in there to take her in his arms and kiss her hungrily. Casey returned his kiss, she couldn't help it, but there was a hint of reserve in her manner as she stepped away from him. 'I've got flour on my hands; I'll mess up your clothes.'

'Who cares?' Reid laughed, too full of hope to notice. 'What are you making?'

'*Boeuf en croûte*. I found the recipe in one of the cookery books I had as a wedding present so I thought I'd try it.'

'Great.' Reid put his arms round her waist and hugged her tightly. 'How about a drink for the chef?'

He went away to get it and for a moment Casey looked bitterly after him before returning to her task. He was so sure of himself again, so certain that he was already half-way to winning that he looked a different man from the one who had gone away so angrily and dejectedly.

After bringing her drink, Reid went upstairs to unpack, then came to join her, chatting about his trip to America and wanting to know everything she had been doing. If he noticed her reserve he refused to acknowledge it, determinedly acting as if nothing was, or ever had been, wrong. The beef turned out OK, which was a relief as Casey had never attempted it before, and Reid was loud in his praise. He seemed happy, as he had been while they were engaged. And somehow to see him happy when she wasn't made her own hurt worse, as if he was being happy at her expense.

She pushed her plate away, the food hardly touched. 'Aren't you hungry?'

'No. Somehow cooking things yourself takes the edge off it.'

After dinner they went into the sitting-room and Reid showed her all the presents he had brought her back from the States: perfume, table napkins, a most unusual photograph frame he had found in an antique shop, and a beautiful silk blouse. She should have revelled in the presents, but Casey could only smile and thank him politely, unable to feel whole-hearted about anything any more. They watched televison and at eleven-thirty went up to bed, Reid making no move to stop her when she went into the spare bedroom.

The following day was Friday, and when Casey got home from the warehouse she found that Reid had everything worked out. She could tell that he was excited about something, although he did his best to suppress it, and he was far too experienced just to blurt out what was on his mind. But it didn't take a lot of guessing and Casey showed no surprise when, after they had eaten, Reid suggested a walk to the local pub, and on the way he told her that he had fixed up to take her into Norfolk on Sunday morning to see a demonstration of the latest safety devices. 'And as it's so near to your home I thought we might go on there afterwards to see how Mark's getting along,' he added as a further inducement.

Casey didn't answer, so after a moment, Reid said persuasively, 'You did say you were willing to talk about it, darling, so I thought I'd fix this up so that you'd know exactly what I was trying to explain to you.'

'Yes, all right,' she agreed dully, dispirited by his eagerness.

But having gained so much, Reid wasn't to be put down by her lack of enthusiasm, and exerted himself to charm her back into a good mood. Eventually he had her laughing again so that, on the surface, it was almost like old times. On Saturday he kept her busy, taking her shopping in London and to a show in the evening so that Casey had no time at all to think. Except when she was alone at night. Then he couldn't stop her from feeling that she was being cowardly, that she was allowing herself to be persuaded into letting her body rule her heart and mind.

They set out at eight o'clock the next morning, stopping for coffee on the way, and arrived by ten-thirty at the Norfolk factory where the Kevlar safety-cells had been invented. The people there greeted Reid like an old friend, but also with a great deal of respect and admiration, and seemed not to mind in the least giving up their Sunday morning for him. Reid introduced her to everyone and, although they were friendly enough on the surface, to Casey, her senses made acute through continual nervous tension, it was obvious that there was reserve underneath. If they hadn't actually been told then they definitely guessed why Reid had brought her, and they were secretly rather scornful of her fears, but willing to do their best to help Reid rather than her.

So they explained everything in great detail while Casey listened politely and watched as they demonstrated the toughness of the safety-cell by dropping heavy weights on it that didn't even dent it. They even got someone to take a boat out and turn it over so that she could see how, when it sank, the flotation chambers brought the nose and the driver's seat up so that he couldn't drown even if he was knocked unconscious. When they had finished they all looked at her expectantly, waiting for her to admit that she had been a fool, but Casey merely smiled and thanked them politely, leaving Reid to say his goodbyes and follow her to the car.

'Do you mind if I drive?' she asked him.

'No, of course not. I'll navigate.'

Reid only spoke to direct her until they came to a straight open road and then he could contain his impatience no longer. 'Well? What did you think?' he demanded eagerly.

'I think the men there wanted you to go on racing as much as you want to,' she answered obliquely.

Some of the eagerness in Reid's face faded. 'So?'

'So, because of that, and because they invented the safety-cell, maybe they were biased in its favour.' She gave him a quick glance. 'Don't you agree that might be so?'

His jaw tightened. 'I suppose that means you didn't believe a word they said? That it's all been a waste of time?'

'No, I didn't mean that.' Striving to keep her voice calm and even, Casey said, 'It all sounds OK—in theory.'

'And in practice,' Reid said urgently, leaning towards her. '*Believe* me, darling. It's been tried and tested, dozens of times. Nearly every Formula One boat in racing has been fitted with them and no one who has used one has been badly hurt.

'All right! You've told me before,' Casey broke in sharply. 'And now I've seen them I'm willing to accept that they are very good, but I . . .'

'Casey! For God's sake, stop this car,' Reid said fiercely.

Startled, she hurriedly obeyed him. 'What is it?'

His face alight, Reid undid his safety-strap and reached out to take her hands. 'Darling, do you mean that you're really convinced at last? That we can . . .'

'No!' Casey cut in hastily. 'I only said in theory. I haven't . . .' She paused, biting her lip. Reid's face had fallen and he waited tensely for her to go on. With a sigh, Casey said, 'When is your next race?'

His eyes studied her face. 'My *next* race?'

'Yes.'

'In about ten days' time.'

'All right, then. Wherever it is, I'll come and watch it. I'll—I'll see for myself.'

With a rather rueful grin Reid raised her hand to his lips and kissed it. 'Well, it's a long way from what I'd hoped, but compared to what we've been going through this last few weeks it's a hell of a step forward. Thank you, sweetheart. I promise you you won't regret it.'

Casey wasn't at all sure about that, but said, 'Where is your next race? When will we have to leave?'

Reid laughed, sounding happier than he had for weeks. 'We won't. The next race is here in England. At the Victoria Docks in London. So I'm afraid you don't get to go abroad, after all—unless you'd like to, that is. We can always . . .'

'No! No, I don't want another—holiday.'

Reaching out, Reid gently smoothed her hair, his eyes on her troubled face. 'My poor darling, you're still far from happy, aren't you? But you will be—and soon. I swear you will be.' And leaning forward, he put his hands on either side of her head to kiss her. It was a long, deep kiss, the type that you can lose yourself in, drown in until everything else is forgotten. Casey emerged from it feeling like a James Bond drink: shaken but not stirred. She managed to smile at him, but immediately started the car again and drove on.

They spent a few hours with her family, finding Mark hopping around on crutches and terribly impatient to get back to racing, wanting to talk to Reid about nothing else. It would have been pleasant but for that, and after a couple of hours of it Casey felt as if she wanted to scream, and abruptly walked out of the room.

For a while it was almost a relief to get home, but when they were going up to bed Reid paused on the landing to take her in his arms and kiss her goodnight. It was a kiss that deepened into passion, his hands moving over her. It reminded Casey of the kisses he had given her when they had been engaged, when they had agreed to wait but knew they were going to go to bed together soon. His hands and lips were sure again, possessive, seeking to dominate her into submission.

With a cry Casey tore herself away from him, pushing at his chest with her hands. 'No, please!'

'But sweetheart, surely we can at least go to bed together now? I won't make you do anything you don't want, but we can hold each other and kiss and—and at least show each other that we're in love.'

'No!' Casey said again vehemently. 'I'm sorry, but I—I can't.'

Reid's mouth twisted sarcastically. 'I see. You're determined to carry this through to the bitter end. And something tells me that it will be bitter—not sweet as it should have been.' He looked at her broodingly. 'Sometimes I wonder if we're ever going to be able to forget this, Casey. Whether we'll ever really be able to put it completely out of our minds.'

That felt like a knife piercing her heart and Casey couldn't take it so she took refuge in flippancy, saying, 'What does it matter? It'll all be the same in a hundred years.'

Reid's face darkened. 'That is an extremely stupid and childish remark,' he said shortly, and turning on his heel went into his room.

He just didn't understand. He thought that she was coming round to his viewpoint, and in a way Casey supposed she was. But only in her mind, because logic was persuading her to do so. In her heart she knew that she would always be afraid for him.

As she lay in bed, staring up at the ceiling, Casey realised that she was hurtling down to a major crossroads in her life. And the road she would take would be decided during Reid's race next week. The easy way, of course, would be to give in, to yield to Reid's persuasion and the overwhelming desires of her own body. But always afterwards, she knew in her subconscious, the reserve that was growing in her would be between them. She would build up a shell to protect herself so that the pain wouldn't be so bad if ever he was hurt. And what kind of a marriage would that be? And then there was the other alternative; if she went on saying no. But Casey's mind still shied away from that one, too afraid to follow it through to its logical conclusion.

Reid, in his glowing optimism, was unaware of the internal barriers that Casey was putting up to protect herself when the time came. Either way, she was going to need them. But she tried desperately to conceal her feelings and succeeded so well that that week was one of the happiest they had ever spent together, not as lovers but as loving friends. Sure in his own mind that he only had that week to wait, Reid managed to control his impatience most of the time, although when they were close like this frustration sometimes threatened to drive him crazy. Then he would groan and hold her very close as if holding her like that could assuage the deep ache in his loins.

He went to London a day ahead of her to prepare for the race, but gave her detailed instructions on how to get there and where to go. 'You will come?' he said anxiously as he was about to leave. 'You'll keep your promise?'

'Yes,' Casey agreed, but there was no warmth in her lips as she kissed him goodbye.

She didn't eat that day, just as she had hardly eaten for the whole week, her stomach tied in tight knots of tension that made food indigestible. By five the next morning she couldn't stay in bed any longer and got up, putting heavy make-up on to disguise the dark circles round her eyes, and dressing carefully in new pale pink jeans and matching jacket, trying to look her best so that Reid would be proud of her.

Casey wasn't used to driving round London's busy one-way streets, but Reid had mapped out the journey very carefully for her and she arrived at the docks a good hour ahead of time, parking in the space that Reid had reserved for her alongside the pits. She sat there for quite a while, thinking back to when they met and nerving herself to get out of the car. Reid had told her to go straight to the pits where he would be waiting, but Casey walked, with the crowds of people who were arriving, towards the race area. She hadn't quite known what to expect, but certainly not this enclosed piece of water between high concrete banks with tiers of seats like grandstands on either side. To her heightened senses it seemed like a giant-sized Roman arena and she wondered with cynical bitterness if that was what the crowds had come in search of: spectacular crashes and blood rather than a contest of skill.

There were marker buoys around the course, and at each end was a boat with a big red cross painted on the roof and sides. Casey saw them and turned blindly away, bumping into people in her hurry.

There was a stall selling drink and Casey bought herself a double brandy, standing there in the sun until she had some control over her shivering body again. Only then did she follow Reid's instructions and go to the pits to find him. He was looking out for her anxiously, worried that she wouldn't come, his frown clearing magically when he caught sight of her. He came hurrying over and put his arm round her waist, 'What happened to you? I was getting worried.'

'There was so much traffic; it took me longer than I thought,' Casey lied.

He was wearing an overall with 'LOMAX POWER-BOATS' written on the back and on the flap of the pocket. He was about to lead her away when some fans, who shouldn't really have been there, rushed up and asked him for his autograph, firing questions and wishes of good luck at him. An official came over and shooed the fans away and Reid was able to take her into his pit and introduce her to his racing team. She had met some of them before at his factory where he was just the boss, but today he had a different status, the team fussing around him and the boat as if they were gods. The boat sat like a crouched animal on the water, just waiting for Reid's touch for it to spring into life, its engine the biggest outboard motor Casey had ever seen. It exuded streamlined power and she had no difficulty in believing that it could get up to a hundred and fifty miles an hour and accelerate faster than a Formula One racing car, as one of the team told her in excited pride, until he caught Reid's frown and took himself off.

'Quite a few of my customers are here today,' Reid told her. 'I've reserved you a seat with them.' He grinned, completely happy now that she was there, a current of excitement running through him at the thought of the race ahead when he would be the favourite contestant in his own country. 'I expect they're having a bit of a party. Would you like to go up and join them?'

Casey shook her head. 'No, I'd rather stay here for a while, if I'm not in the way.'

'You're never in the way,' he assured her with a kiss. Somebody called him and he raised a hand in acknowledgement. 'I have to get ready. Wish me luck?'

'Oh, *yes*.' She hugged him fiercely, not wanting to let him go, so that he had to take her arms from round his neck.

'I'll be all right,' he assured her. 'You'll see, darling. *Trust me*.'

She nodded, her face white, and watched as he put on a life-jacket and an open-fronted crash-helmet. Then he climbed into the cockpit of the boat and did up the safety-harness. Reid turned to grin and give her a thumbs-up sign before the huge, brain-burstingly noisy engine sprang into life. She watched as Reid took the boat out on to the water for a couple of warm-up laps, and was just turning to go and find her seat when a girl from the next-door pit who had been watching her came over. 'Hi,' she said in a strong North American accent. 'Are you Reid's new wife?'

'Yes, that's right.'

'Well, we were all wondering when you'd finally show up at a race. Don't you like travelling or something?'

'We?' Casey asked, avoiding the question.

'All the wives and girlfriends. We all get to know one another from following our men around the Grand Prix circuit.'

'Oh, I see.'

She went to move on, but the girl said curiously, 'Is this your first race?'

'Yes. Yes, it is.'

'Well, say, why don't you come sit with me? My name's Jan Greenburg.'

'Thank you,' Casey agreed, much preferring to sit through the race with another woman. 'Mine's Casey.' She followed the other girl to some seats just above the pits. 'Is your husband taking part?'

Jan's bright face darkened. 'No, he crashed at the end of last year and he's still hospitalised back home.'

'He crashed?' Casey stared at her in horror.

'Yes, but he was lucky. At least he didn't get killed. Four Formula One pilots were killed in five Grand Prix races a couple of seasons ago. One of them drowned and that's why they wear open helmets now; it takes eight seconds for a visor to empty of water and the driver drowned before they could get to him.' She paused, then added, 'A Formula One motor racing driver tried it once and described it as like racing a car across a ploughed field at full speed.'

Casey's stomach muscles tightened in terror and she looked out over the circuit to where the twenty brightly coloured power-boats were doing their warm-up laps, the crowds of people in the full, sunlit grandstands already shouting encouragement.

'I hate leaving Jeff in hospital,' Jan was saying, 'but I act as secretary to our racing team, and we could do with the money.'

'Was—was your husband badly injured?'

'Wow, I'll say!' The American girl launched into a list of his injuries. 'His larynx is permanently wired together and he may never speak above a loud whisper again. He has lacerated fingers on both hands . . .'

The engine noise of the boats died for a moment as they all waited in line at the start. Then the traffic-light starting-system changed to green and they simultaneously rocketed down the straight towards the first turn buoy, dense clouds of spray flying up behind them.

For a moment Jan's voice was almost drowned out, but Casey could hear it in the background telling of a crushed heel and lacerated foot. The boats surged down to the buoy, all converging on it together and fighting to get the inside position.

'. . . stretched plexus nerve in his right arm . . . very painful . . . constant throbbing . . .'

Jan's voice droned on as Casey watched fixedly. Some of the boats were round but she couldn't see if one was Reid's. Then two boats must have touched, because one spun wildly.

'. . . cast on his leg for three months . . .'

Casey had got to her feet, biting on her hand as she watched the boat spin and crash against the dock wall. It was a blue boat. Reid's boat wasn't blue, it was white. It wasn't Reid. The boat didn't sink and within seconds a red cross rescue boat was alongside it, keeping well out of the way of the other nineteen boats that were obliviously still going round the circuit at top speed, the field more spread out now.

But Casey had seen and heard as much as she could take. A terrible griping pain filled her stomach, and she turned and ran. Ran until she found a women's Portaloo and went inside to be horribly sick, her body retching painfully. She stood there for a long time, leaning against the thin wall of the cabin, beads of perspiration on her face, her breath coming in shuddering, sobbing pants. When she managed to leave the lavatory and go to the basin to wash her face, the attendant gave her a sympathetic look. 'You pregnant, dearie?' she asked.

'No.' Casey looked down at her hand where she had bitten it so hard that the blood had flowed. 'No, I'm not pregnant.'

She wrapped a handkerchief round her hand and somehow found her way back to the car, driving slowly all the way home in a numb kind of limbo where all her senses were functioning perfectly well, but her spirit was completely detached from it.

Back at the Victoria Dock, Reid swept past the chequered flag, first again, and after he had done his lap of honour came happily into the pits, his eyes searching for Casey. 'Where's my wife?' he demanded as soon as he stepped out of the boat.

The men looked uncomfortable, but then the senior man said, 'I'm sorry, Reid; we saw her get into her car and drive away less than half-way through the race.'

The excitement and happiness of winning drained from Reid's face. He strode through the pits to see the empty space for himself, then began to tear off his helmet and life-jacket.

'But Reid, what about the victory ceremony?' one of the men exclaimed.

His face grim, Reid said fiercely, 'To hell with it! I've got more important things to do.'

As soon as she reached the house Casey went up to the bedroom and began to pack her suitcases, putting things in haphazardly, still too numb really to think what she was doing. In the back of her mind she knew that before she left she was going to have to sit down and write Reid a letter, somehow convince him that she had tried, really tried, but just couldn't go on any longer.

As she packed, half her brain worried over the letter, but the other half kept remembering that boat spinning round and how easily it could have been Reid's, until nausea overcame her again and she had to go to the bathroom, although her stomach was empty now and there was only pain and wretchedness.

She had just come out of the bathroom and had started to pack again when Reid got there. He had driven fast and screeched to a stop outside, not bothering to shut any doors as he ran in and up the stairs. One smouldering glance took in the whole situation.

'What the hell do you think you're doing?' he shouted angrily as he strode murderously towards her.

'Reid, I've got to go. I . . .'

'You're not going anywhere!' Sweeping her clothes from the case he threw them on the floor, then picked up the case and threw that violently after them.

'Oh, Reid, I tried. But I couldn't watch. I couldn't stay!' Casey raised her hands to her face in distress.

'You coward! You were running out on me. If I hadn't come right after you you'd have been gone. Without a word. Just gone! Left me.'

'No, I was going to leave you a note. I . . .'

'A note!' His mouth twisting with fury, Reid caught hold of her wrists, dragging them down from her face. 'I never thought that you'd go this far to try and force my hand. But it seems that there's a hell of a lot I'm learning about you lately.' His teeth gritted, he went on fiercely, 'I really thought that you were beginning to see reason, that we were getting somewhere. I even thought that tonight—tonight . . .' His voice broke and his head went down on his chest, his powerful hands almost crushing her wrists as he strove to control himself.

Her heart wrung at the agony in his face, Casey cried, 'Oh Reid, don't, please! I'm sorry, I'm so desperately sorry. But you must see that I can't stay. It wouldn't be honest to stay now.'

Reid suddenly straightened up, letting go of her wrists to shake her. 'You're just putting on the pressure to make me give up racing. It's just more blackmail, more . . .'

'No!' Casey yelled, trying to break through his anger. 'No. I've seen you now. I know how much you love it. I'm not asking you to give it up any more. Because I know you can't. But you're right; I'm a coward. I can't take the stress of watching you or even knowing that you're going to race and might be hurt. So I have to leave, can't you see that?'

'No! I'm here. I'm alive. You should have stayed.'

'I saw a boat crash.'

Reid made an angrily dismissive gesture. 'That was nothing. His engine was damaged, that was all. No one was hurt.'

But Casey pushed past him and made for the door, knowing that to go on arguing was useless. 'Where are you going?'

'I don't know. Anywhere.'

'No, you're not.' He grabbed her and pulled her back. 'What's the use of talking? There's only one way to settle this and I should have done it weeks ago.' Picking her up Reid carried her across his shoulder to the bed and dropped her on it, coming down on top of her to stop her getting away.

But Casey didn't try to fight, she just lay there as he tore off her jacket and then her shirt, the buttons flying because he was too angry to undo them. She lay still, biting her lip, as his hot hands touched her breasts then impatiently moved on to tear at the fastening of her jeans and pull them off. 'Is this what you want?' Reid shouted at her. 'Do you want me to force you? Is that what you've wanted all along?' His hands went over her avidly, but for the first time she was able to control her erring body and not respond.

Lifting an angry hand to the neck of his overall, Reid began to pull down the zip, but stopped as he finally became aware of her stillness. He stared down at her as Casey said, in deep sadness, 'No, you don't have to force me. You could have taken me at any time. I'm always willing—I can't help myself. It's been just as much torture for me as it has for you. I want to be loved by you—so very much.' Her voice faltered but she went on, 'But I only had to think how much greater a torture it would be if you were killed and I had to go on living without you.'

Slowly Reid stood up and put his hands on the bedpost, his knuckles showing white. It was a couple of minutes before he could control himself enough to speak, but then he said, 'One minute I want to love you, the next I want to hurt you, punish you for what you're doing to us. I'm sure if we could just make love, just once . . .'

But Casey had got off the bed and was putting on some clothes.

'No,' he said, becoming angry again. 'I won't let you go.'

'But you must,' Casey insisted with a note of finality in her tone. 'This—situation isn't doing either of us any good. We have to be apart for a while, to—to simmer down and think clearly. Maybe then we can talk again, figure out what we're going to do.'

'Then I'll go,' Reid said in wretched acceptance. 'You must stay here.'

'No, this is your home. Please, I'd—I'd rather go. You can—you can tell people I've gone to see my parents if anyone asks.'

'Casey, don't do this, please.' Reid made one last attempt to stop her, reaching urgently out to take her in his arms.

But Casey held him off. 'No. Can't you see that that only makes it harder? It always has. I'm so sorry, Reid, sorry that I wasn't the kind of wife you wanted.' And she turned and ran out of the room, leaving him staring bleakly after her.

Casey didn't go home to her parents, instead she found a bed and breakfast place in the town where the warehouse was situated. At a time when she knew he would be out she went over to the house and collected her clothes, leaving Reid a note telling him where she was staying. She spent most of the time at the warehouse unit and

Reid phoned her there, but she firmly told him not to do so again unless it was urgent.

'It is urgent,' he replied forcefully. 'You're my wife and I want you back.'

'Reid, you're trying to rush me and it won't work. You've got to give me time.'

'Time for what?'

But he had allowed her to persuade him against his better judgement, although in her heart Casey knew that he was right; she didn't really need any more time. In her mind she had left him; it was over and she should never have married him. It was Reid who needed time to get used to the idea, to realise that it was over, too.

Another heat-wave hit the south of England; in England any hot weather that lasts more than a week automatically becomes a heat-wave, the perverse nature of the Britsh immediately making them long for rain. It was sweltering too in the warehouse, but Casey hated her digs and stayed at work until the caretaker turned her out at nine every night. Johnny, next door, suffered even more from the heat as he laboured over his stained glass, using a burner to melt the solder holding the pieces together. They were so hot that they went fifty/fifty on a second-hand fridge so that at least they could have a cold drink whenever they wanted one.

The unit on the other side of her was being developed now and the workmen made a lot of noise, especially when they realised they had a young, good-looking blonde nearby to tease. But Casey took no notice of them, too wrapped up in her own troubles to care.

One morning, about two weeks after she had left Reid, Casey arrived at the warehouse to find some of the workmen outside, stripped down to shorts, all of them tanned by the sun. They were in the process of hauling some machinery up to the unit next to hers on the second floor, using ropes to pull it up the outside rather than struggle with it up the stairs. This unit was a corner one with windows on both walls, whereas hers only overlooked the river so that her knitting-machines had been carried up.

Ignoring their wolf-whistles and suggestive remarks, Casey went up to her own unit and, as she did every morning, went to lean far out of the window to look back along the river to where she could just see the head of the lake, feeling that it was a line that somehow still linked her to Reid.

She set to work, doing so automatically and with no real interest, but making the sweaters beautifully all the same, because she was basically efficient. It was very hot, the sun moving to shine in her window in the afternoon when it was at its hottest. Johnny gave up and went down to sleep and sunbathe on the grass outside, coming up again to carry on when it was cooler. Casey could hear him whistling tunelessly, as he always did when he was concentrating, long after most of the other people there had gone home. At eight-thirty she banged on the wall and he came round for a drink, standing chatting with her for a good half-hour until they decided to pack up and go home.

'I'm surprised the caretaker hasn't been round,' Casey remarked.

'He's probably round the pub having a drink, too.'

Johnny went out and Casey went over to close her window, taking a last look towards the lake and then staring in open-mouthed dismay. There was smoke pouring from Johnny's window. She ran to the door just as he came through it, coughing, his hand over his mouth.

She grabbed his arm. 'Come on, let's get out.'

But he pulled her back. 'It's no good,' he got out between coughs. 'We can't get down the stairs. They're impassable.' He gave her a haunted look. 'Oh God, I think I must have left my burner going.'

Casey stared at him, appalled. 'The fire brigade!' She ran to the phone and gave a prayer of relief when it was still working. Quickly she rang and explained where they were, that they couldn't get out. Then she ran to the window. 'Could we jump into the river, if we had to?'

'These ceilings are high, it must be about fifty feet and it hasn't rained for ages so the water will be low. If we jump we could kill ourselves.'

'A rope, then. If we had a rope we could lower ourselves down on the pulley they used for the flour.'

'But we haven't got one,' Johnny answered in despair.

It was very hot and they both suddenly realised that the heat was coming through the wall, not from the sun any more, and that wall was the one that Casey stored all her yarns against.

'The unit next door,' Casey exclaimed, fear forcing her brain to work. 'They were using some ropes this morning. If they're still there . . .'

Johnny nodded in hopeful eagerness. 'I'll go and have a look.'

'Here, put something over your mouth.'

They soaked a piece of a sweater in Coca Cola and Johnny went out, shutting the door behind him to keep the smoke out. It was a solid door and Casey could hear nothing through it. If Johnny didn't come back . . . Without even thinking about it Casey went again to the phone, instinct telling her that Reid would be doing the same as her and trying to appease the hurt by working late at the marina.

He answered at once, but it was a moment before she could find her voice. 'Casey, is that you?' he asked urgently.

'Yes. Reid, there's a fire at the warehouse. I'm—I'm trapped. With Johnny. He's trying to find a rope. I just want you to know in—in case, that I love you so very much.'

But he just said, 'I'm coming,' and dropped the phone. She could hear him shouting to someone, his voice fading.

For a long moment Casey stood gripping the phone, thinking of all the things that could have been, but then Johnny was back, his face and clothes blackened, but triumphantly carrying a long rope.

'Oh, well done! Well done!' Casey hugged him and dragged the rope over to the window. Dimly she heard the sound of fire engines growing nearer as she leaned out. The river looked an awful long way down. 'Can you thread the rope through the pulley?' she called to Johnny.

He came to the window to see, but then drew back, his face draining of colour beneath the black smudges. 'I'm sorry, Casey, but I can't stand heights. I get dizzy.'

'All right, it doesn't matter. I'll do it. You hold the other end of the rope.' She pushed the window wider and a gush of smoke blew in her face, making her cough. There were flames coming out of Johnny's window now and she could hear the small explosions of breaking glass. Opposite, on the other side of the river, was another, lower warehouse, too far away to be any use and with too narrow a strip of ground in front of it for a fire engine to get up and put its ladder across. But some men had run along and seen her, and were shouting to the firemen.

Grimly Casey stepped out on to the narrow ledge below the window and worked her way to the pulley, then lowered herself to sit astride it while she threaded the rope through, just praying that it was still solid enough to take her weight. 'All right, it's through,' she called to Johnny.

'OK, tie the end round your waist and I'll lower you down.'

'What about you, will you be able to climb down?'

'Yes, of course. Go on, go. It's getting hot in here.'

Hastily Casey tied the rope. 'I'll abseil. I did it once on an adventure holiday.'

'OK. Ready?' She nodded and Johnny said, 'Sorry I ruined your business,' and took the strain of the rope as she began to go down. Half-way it occurred to Casey that she was going to walk straight into the river, but then she heard the noise of an engine above the shouts of encouragement from the crowd of people who were watching and she saw a power-boat surging up the river towards her. An open boat with Lomax Marine painted on the side.

Reid reached her as she dangled a yard above the water and brought the boat under her so that he could just reach up and help her inside. He took the rope off then held her very, very tightly, his face buried in her neck. But then the people on the bank stopped cheering and began to shout and one of the two men Reid had brought with him said, 'That other chap isn't coming down.'

Turning, Casey looked up again at the warehouse to see that Johnny had half climbed out of the window, but was going back again—and there was smoke coming out of there now, too!

'Oh no! He's afraid of heights. He isn't going to make it! Johnny, come on,' she yelled. 'You can do it.'

Again Johnny tried, but this time he could only stand on the ledge holding on to the window-frame, unable to move.

'He's frozen!' Reid exclaimed. 'I'll go up and get him.'

For a moment Casey's wide, frightened eyes met his, but she made no attempt to stop him. Reid grinned at her, then took hold of the rope and began to climb.

The people on the bank began to shout and cheer again and there was even the flash of cameras, but Casey watched in silent fear as Reid went higher towards the billowing smoke, mixed with flames now, that came from her window. It was more difficult to negotiate the pulley going up than going down, but he managed it and stood up beside Johnny, tying the rope under his armpits and somehow persuading him to release his iron grip on the window and lowering him down.

'Oh, quickly, quickly,' Casey prayed, watching the flames spreading. It seemed light years before Johnny was safely in the boat, then Reid was immediately on the rope again himself, sliding down it to jump down beside Johnny who still had his eyes tightly shut.

'Look out,' someone yelled and they just had time to move out of the way as the burning rope fell and was quickly thrown into the water. Casey looked at it, smouldering and sizzling, then looked up again at the warehouse, the whole floor engulfed now by flames. She began to shake and Reid gave an order to the helmsman, who took them further along to where the fire appliances were.

A fireman ran over to them. 'Is anyone else inside?'

'The caretaker; I don't know where he is,' Casey exclaimed, remembering.

'He's all right. He wasn't even in there.'

There was an ambulance standing by and they put Johnny inside to take him to hospital for burns to his hand and for shock. The ambulance man wanted her to go too, but Casey looked at Reid and shook her head. 'No, I'm all right. I'd rather go home.'

So they took the boat back along the lake to the mooring below the house and Reid insisted on carrying her to the house and up to his bedroom. There he gently undressed her and bathed her with his own hands, washing off the smoke and smell of fire from her soft skin. He found her a pair of his pyjamas and put her in his bed, looking down at her for a long, tender moment before going to bathe himself.

When he came back into the bedrom with a big bath towel wrapped round him, Casey was awake, waiting.

Sitting down on the edge of the bed Reid picked up her hand to kiss her fingers. 'You should try and sleep.'

'No, I had to thank you. For what you did for Johnny. And for—for coming.'

'Oh, my darling! How could you possibly think I wouldn't come?' His grip on her hand tightened. 'But when I think of you trapped up there . . . It's made me see things a whole lot clearer. Maybe that's what I've needed; to feel what it's like when someone you love is in danger. I was going through all kinds of hell during that ride in the boat. If what you feel whenever I race is even the half of that, then I have no right to put you through such torment. I've never cared for myself, but if anything happened to you . . .' He gave a short laugh. 'I've been a selfish bastard, haven't I? Wanting the best of both worlds. But my last race really was my last; I won't race again. You don't have to be afraid any more, my love. You're all that matters to me.'

'Oh, Reid.' Tears came to her eyes and Casey held his hand tightly against her cheek. 'I think that is the most wonderful thing you'll ever say to me. But maybe I learned something tonight, too,' she added huskily. 'If you hadn't been the brave, reckless kind of man you are, you'd never have gone up that rope, and Johnny would have died. I know that I can't change you, Reid, and now I know that I don't want to. I don't want you at home eating your heart out for the sport you love. I—I don't know that I'll ever be brave enough to watch you, but I want you to promise me that you'll go on racing until *you're* ready to give up.' She smiled. 'Oh, and you must promise to keep on winning, of course.'

Reid stared at her. 'You really mean it, don't you?' She nodded and he hugged her happily. 'And you'll move back here tomorrow?'

She looked rueful. 'Well, I don't think I'll be going into work.'

'Not for some time, I'm afraid. But never mind, it will give us the opportunity to have that honeymoon we missed while you wait for the insurance money to come through.'

Casey lay back on the pillows. 'I'd like that.'

He stroked her hair. 'You'd better go to sleep. You've had quite a night.'

He stood up, but Casey said, 'Do you have to go?'

A great light shone in Reid's eyes. 'Are you saying what I think you're saying?'

Pulling back the bedclothes, Casey said huskily, 'Why

don't you come in and find out?'

Reid took off the bath-towel and climbed in beside her, and lay looking at her for a long moment. 'I was right,' he said thickly. 'It is going to be quite a night.' And he reached out to start undoing the buttons of her pyjamas.

'I thought you said you never wear pyjamas,' Casey remarked, her pulses already beginning to race.

'I don't. Elaine made me buy them to take on honeymoon, in case——' a big grin spread over his face '—in case there was ever a fire!'

They both laughed, until Reid's eyes darkened and he said, 'Come here, wife.'

'Oh yes, *please*,' Casey agreed fervently and went happily into his arms at last.

Harlequin Presents

Coming Next Month

Available in October wherever paperback books are sold, or through Harlequin Reader Service:

In the U.S.
901 Fuhrmann Blvd.
P.O. Box 1397
Buffalo, N.Y. 14240-1397

In Canada
P.O. Box 603
Fort Erie, Ontario
L2A 5X3

Temptation™

TEMPTATION WILL BE
EVEN HARDER TO RESIST...

In September, Temptation is presenting a sophisticated new face to the world. A fresh look that truly brings Harlequin's most intimate romances into focus.

What's more, all-time favorite authors Barbara Delinsky, Rita Clay Estrada, Jayne Ann Krentz and Vicki Lewis Thompson will join forces to help us celebrate. The result? A very special quartet of Temptations...

- **Four striking covers**
- **Four stellar authors**
- **Four sensual love stories**
- **Four variations on one spellbinding theme**

All in one great month! Give in to Temptation in September.

HARLEQUIN SIGNATURE EDITION

VIOLET WINSPEAR

HOUSE OF STORMS

Editorial secretary Debra Hartway travels to the Salvador family's rugged Cornish island home to work on Jack Salvador's latest book. Disturbing questions hang in the troubled air over Lovelis Island. What or who had caused the tragic death of Jack's young wife? Why did Jack stay away from the home and, more especially, the baby son he loved so well? And—why should Rodare, Jack's brother, who had proved himself a man of the highest integrity, constantly invade Debra's thoughts with such passionate, dark desires . . .?

Violet Winspear, who has written more than 65 romance novels translated worldwide into 18 languages, is one of Harlequin's best-loved and bestselling authors. HOUSE OF STORMS, her second title in the Harlequin Signature Edition program, is a full-length novel rich in romantic tradition and intriguingly spiced with an atmosphere of danger and mystery.

Watch for HOUSE OF STORMS—coming in October!

HOFS-1